A DOCTOR'S PROMISE

LAURA SCOTT

READSCAPE PUBLISHING, LLC

1

*S*ymptoms range from stunted growth to multisystem organ failure and ultimately death.

The words echoed over and over in her mind like a mantra. Flight nurse Shelly Bennett slipped unnoticed from the debriefing area, seeking the relative peace and quiet of Lifeline's lounge. She sank onto the sofa and rubbed a hand over her gritty, bloodshot eyes. Nausea still churned in her stomach four days after learning about her five-year-old son's abnormal lab values. As a result of hearing the news, she'd stayed up late every night, surfing online and devouring every bit of information she could find on pediatric renal failure.

She closed her eyes against an overwhelming surge of helplessness. *Please, God, he's just a little boy. Please keep Tyler healthy.*

"Good morning."

Her eyes snapped open at the deep male greeting. A tall, blond-haired stranger with a square jaw and brilliant blue eyes, wearing a one-piece navy blue flight suit exactly like hers, stood a few feet away. Shelly frowned and quickly stood. Who was this guy? Had she missed something over the past few days in her concerned haze over Ty?

The stranger didn't seem to notice her confusion. "Ah, I was hoping to find fresh coffee here."

"Good morning, Jared." Kate, one of her fellow flight nurses, entered the debriefing room. Fluffing her short blond curls, Kate stepped forward with a bright smile. "How was your move from Boston? Are you finally settled?"

"I still have things in boxes, but for the most part, I'm moved in. The condo is very nice and affordable compared to Boston." He helped himself to a cup of coffee from a pot on a nearby counter, then turned toward Shelly, extending his free hand. "I don't believe we've met. Jared O'Connor, new Medical Director here at Lifeline Air Rescue."

Oh yes, she remembered now. Shelly nodded and forced a smile as she took his hand in greeting. Despite her worry over her son, a tingle of awareness skipped down her spine as she shook hands with her new boss. Dr. Jared O'Connor's palm radiated a gentle strength as it held hers, and she found herself oddly reluctant to let go.

His distinct East Coast accent reminded her of Ty's father's family, especially since Mark's last name had been O'Connor, too. She'd encountered one other O'Connor in recent years, no relation to Mark. This was likely the same situation, but the coincidence jolted her just the same.

Abruptly nervous, she cleared her throat. "Shelly Bennett, Flight Nurse. Pleased to meet you, Dr. O'Connor. Welcome to Lifeline."

"I'm happy to be here, but please, call me Jared." He eyed her over the rim of his cup. "Shelly. You're one of the pediatric nurses, aren't you?"

She flushed at his intent perusal, wondering if she'd

somehow betrayed her unexpected flash of awareness. "Yes."

"Good to hear, my expertise is pediatrics, too. Explains why we've been paired to fly together."

"Lucky duck," Kate muttered under her breath.

"Great." Shelly tried to hide her inner dismay. This was the worst time for her long-ignored hormones to wake up over some man. There was only room for one male in her life, her son Tyler. Unfortunately, Lifeline was small enough to make avoiding the handsome doctor difficult. Knowing they both worked pediatrics made it practically impossible. Being stuck in the sardine-like confines of the helicopter with Jared O'Connor was a complication she didn't need.

Was it possible he was related to Mark's family? Trying to control a flash of panic, she searched his features for a sign of family resemblance. She'd only met Mark's parents once and that was more than enough, thank you very much. Mark hadn't gotten along with his family very well. No big surprise there.

Mark had brown hair, golden brown eyes, and a light-hearted attitude toward life. Jared's blue eyes were solemn, his blond hair thick. He was taller than Mark and more than just physically attractive—there was an intensity about him that called to her on a very basic level. Her unwelcome reaction was so foreign, she took an automatic step back, nearly tripping over the sofa behind her.

Squaring her shoulders, she forced herself to think logically and to ignore Jared's subtle attempt to grab her if she had fallen. There were hundreds of O'Connors in Boston. Mark's father was a lawyer; in fact, Mark had been in law school when they'd first met.

Before he'd died.

Calmer now, she relaxed, keenly aware of how Jared

watched her. Their previous medical director, Dr. Frank Holmes, had been from Boston, too. No doubt Jared O'Connor's presence here was a result of his working with Holmes in the past, nothing more.

Now if she could just ignore her ridiculous attraction to him, she'd be fine. Honestly, she needed to get a grip. She subtly searched for a wedding ring, hoping Jared was happily married and completely unavailable.

"Can either of you give me some idea which restaurants are good around here?" His question included her and Kate, but his gaze didn't leave Shelly's. "I'm not big on cooking for myself."

"Oh, is your wife moving later, then?" Kate's wide gaze belied her innocent question.

"I'm not married." His tone didn't invite questions.

Shelly's hopes plummeted and crashed to the floor at her feet. So much for him being unavailable. She pasted a smile on her face and hoped her warring dismay and attraction didn't show.

"Well, there's lots of places to eat, La Fluentes if you like Mexican . . ." Kate continued enumerating various restaurants, blatantly announcing her interest in easing his solitude.

Jared's gaze finally unlatched from Shelly's and swung toward Kate. Shelly let out a soundless sigh of relief, grateful for her co-worker's outgoing nature. No doubt Jared would be more interested in a cute willowy blonde than a round, curvy rather plain brunette like herself. She glanced at her watch and noted it was almost time for their training session. Edging toward the door, Shelly figured she'd better head out to the hangar to make sure their pilot Reese Jarvis had everything ready.

She wasn't needed here.

Kate Lawrence held Jared O'Connor in the palms of her very capable hands.

JARED FROWNED when Shelly slipped away, leaving him with the loquacious blonde. Thankfully, Kate's name was printed in block letters on her name tag secured next to the gold wings of her flight suit or he might have forgotten it.

"Thanks for the information." He took another sip of his coffee and glanced at the door Shelly had disappeared through. "I missed morning report but noticed there's a training class scheduled today."

"Yes. Because we're affiliated with the medical school, we teach several emergency-trauma classes to the new residents coming on board. As flight nurses, we get first crack at them, before we turn their very green hides over to you." Kate smiled, and he was abruptly struck by how young she was. She was so full of life she reminded him painfully of his younger brother. Mark had been the same way, intent on living life to its fullest. At least until the moment he'd driven his car at the estimated insane speed of eighty-five miles an hour into a concrete freeway divider.

Pushing aside the constant ache of guilt, Jared followed Kate outside. "Hope you don't mind if I watch."

"Of course not!" Kate looked pleased. "It's a beautiful September day, may as well enjoy it while we can."

His gaze instinctively sought out Shelly. There was something about the pediatric flight nurse that intrigued him. Maybe it was the air of fragility in her heart-shaped face. Or the sorrow darkening her pretty green eyes that made him wonder who or what had put those shadows there.

Kate reminded him of his brother, but Shelly was more like him. Her eyes were mirrors of deep anguish, heartache, and loss.

Similar chords resonated in his heart.

Jared didn't bother listening as Kate rambled on about the training they were preparing to do. His attention was riveted on Shelly who was speaking quietly to Reese, the pilot on duty today. Were the two of them close? He frowned, staring at them intently. There was nothing in the way they stood together to suggest anything other than friendship. Shelly didn't wear a wedding band—not that the absence of a ring meant much these days. Still, he couldn't imagine a woman as beautiful as Shelly not having a man in her life. If not Reese, then someone else.

Why did he care? He was a loner, always had been. More so since that horrible crash six years ago that had taken his brother's life.

His fault. Jared had learned to live with the knowledge that his argument with Mark had caused his brother's death. The gut-wrenching guilt wasn't fresh but existed deep in his soul, a constant ache that would never go away.

There was nothing he could do to give Mark his life back, but he could dedicate his life to saving others. And to finding Mark's runaway fiancée and child.

But that wasn't the only reason he'd traveled halfway across the country. He'd worked with Frank Holmes, the former medical director of Lifeline, during his residency. When Frank's position had become available, he'd jumped at the chance to take it. Director positions of medical transport operations didn't open up on a regular basis. The fact that the position was in Milwaukee, Wisconsin, was an added plus.

His hope of finding Leigh Wilson was slim, but he

wouldn't give up. Not the way their useless private investigator had. Milwaukee wasn't as big as Boston, but trying to find Leigh Wilson would be akin to looking for a needle in a haystack. A cliché? Yep. But accurate all the same.

Restaurants were a place to start. Leigh had been working as a cocktail waitress at Stephan's, an elite club in Boston when she'd met his brother. Six years was a long time, but the one thing the PI had confirmed was that Leigh Wilson had moved to Milwaukee.

And then had disappeared.

It was the only lead he had. The idea of a single mom, struggling to make ends meet without the benefit of a college education, gnawed at him. Mark hadn't spoken much about the woman he'd wanted to marry, and Jared wished he'd pushed for more.

His attention was snagged by a group of four residents, split equally male and female, entering the hangar. Kate and Shelly greeted them and introduced themselves.

"Welcome to Lifeline." Shelly took the lead. "First, the basics. Lifeline provides a transport service with two helicopters and one ground transport vehicle. We log over a thousand flights per year. You will need to pass several classroom training sessions prior to being allowed to fly. Each of your flights will be performed under the supervision of an attending MD until you've been approved by that attending to fly solo."

Distracted by the gentle curve of Shelly's neck, he stopped listening. She was unconsciously graceful. His blood simmered, responding to the picture she made. Confident in her position, yet seemingly vulnerable at the same time, her smile was sweet but never quite met her eyes. Dark brown hair waved gently around her shoulders. He curled his fingers into fists, wishing he had the right to find out if her hair was as soft and silky as it looked.

He averted his gaze. What was he thinking? Women in general were off-limits, but Shelly Bennett in particular. It wasn't smart to date women you worked with.

Besides, he didn't have room in his life for a woman. Not unless that female happened to be Leigh Wilson.

And even then, all he wanted was to meet her and her child. His long-lost niece or nephew.

THE CALL CAME in just as Shelly wrapped up her portion of the resident training session.

"Shelly, we're up." Jared waved her over.

"What's the call?" She jogged to his side.

"Eight-year-old girl with severe hypothermia. She's up at Cedar Bluff, and they're requesting an immediate transfer to Children's Memorial."

There was no time to be nervous about her first flight with her new boss. She nodded, and they both hurried into the hangar.

Reese already had the chopper revved up and ready to go. Jared grabbed his helmet and ducked inside. She followed, closing the lightweight aluminum door behind them. Once their helmets were connected to the intercom, they listened as Reese briefed them on the weather conditions. The interior of the helicopter was tight but compact, the small shelves lining the walls were stuffed with medical supplies. Everything had a place, which was helpful when dealing with emergencies. They buckled themselves into the parallel twin seats.

The ear-splitting drone of the engine, muffled by the

helmet she wore, had the strange effect of making Shelly hyperaware of Jared's presence beside her. He seemed larger, with broader shoulders than any other doctor she'd worked with. When he shifted in his seat, his elbow bumped into hers. She tried to make herself smaller, hunching her shoulders and clasping her hands in her lap, giving Jared plenty of room.

Neither spoke, although their helmets contained microphones and headsets specifically designed for communication. Her gut clenched as the chopper rose from the landing pad and then banked in a steep curve. She'd been flying for two years, but the sensation never failed to give her a thrill. Adrenaline zipped through her bloodstream, and she forced herself to relax and focus on their mission.

Specializing in peds had been her choice long ago. But now, with her son's illness lingering in the back of her mind, she couldn't help but wonder if she could maintain her objectivity. Sick kids were difficult yet usually very rewarding to take care of.

If she could keep her emotions in check.

She shivered, hoping the eight-year-old girl would remain stable until they arrived.

The trip seemed to take forever instead of twenty minutes. When they landed, Shelly was surprised when Jared helped pull the gurney out of the hatch. Many of the doctors didn't bother with menial tasks. They both ditched their helmets and then ran alongside the gurney as they headed inside.

"Thanks for getting here so quickly." A harried female doctor greeted them from the young girl's ICU bedside. "Amy Rawson fell off her family's boat into Lake Michigan. Thankfully, she was wearing a lifejacket, but despite warm September weather, the water barely gets above fifty-five degrees. She was in the water for thirty minutes, and her core temp is dangerously low. We intubated her and put a warmer on. But she's not doing well."

Shelly swallowed hard and went to work switching everything over to their portable equipment. The girl's parents were at the bedside, the mother sobbing as her husband held her tightly. Shelly identified only too well with the mother's pain. It took all of Shelly's concentration to block a sharp wave of empathy and focus only on Amy.

The girl was small, barely thirty-two kilos. Shelly slid an arm under Amy's bony shoulders to help move her. Jared broke off his conversation with the critical care physician and reached over to help. His fingers brushed hers as they seamlessly shifted Amy to the gurney.

There was no reason on earth to be so aware of the purely accidental touch of Jared's hand. Annoyed, she fastened the safety straps with a decisive click.

"Ready?" Jared glanced at her questioningly.

She nodded. "You have the transfer paperwork?"

"Yeah. Let's go." He pushed the gurney forward.

"Wait! We want to come with you!" Amy's mother broke free of her husband, clutching the frame of the gurney as if to hold her daughter there.

"I'm sorry." Jared's gaze softened with regret. "Our policy prevents you from flying with us. Frankly, there isn't enough room. You need to let us take care of your daughter. I promise you can see her as soon as you get to Children's Memorial."

Shelly's heart broke when the mother's face crumpled. She understood the woman's anguish only too well. If the situation were reversed, there would be no way she'd let her son go off alone without a fight.

Amy's father grasped his wife's shoulders and pulled her

close. "Shh, it's okay. We'll drive down. Give us time to pull ourselves together. Amy needs us to be strong, Grace. She needs us to be there for her."

At least Amy's mother wasn't facing this on her own, Shelly thought as she tucked the warming blanket more closely around Amy's shoulders.

In wordless agreement, she and Jared wheeled Amy through the hospital to the elevator that would take them to the helipad. Once they stored Amy safely inside the chopper, they donned their helmets and jumped in beside her. Jared gave the thumbs-up sign to Reese who quickly lifted off.

They worked together as if they'd been doing this for years rather than for the first time. Jared's spicy aftershave pierced the usual scent of jet fuel.

"Core temp up to thirty-two point five," she informed him to the headset. "I've switched to warmed IV fluids."

"Her pulse is still irregular. I'm double-checking the vent settings but get the defib ready."

"It's ready." Shelly's own heart began to beat faster as she confirmed lead placement, then hit the charge button, just in case.

Jared's expression of deep concern, without a hint of arrogance, forced her to acknowledge he was an amazing physician. She stared at Amy's pale, yet perfectly formed features. Her son's face held the same sweet innocence.

Doubt plagued her. If Tyler's next set of testing proved he was suffering from renal failure, could she continue to handle working with sick children?

Or would she constantly imagine her son's face transposed on the features of every child she transported?

2

J ared was secretly amazed at how easy it was to work with Shelly. She anticipated what he needed before he had to ask for it. Clearly, she was exceptionally bright or very experienced, although she didn't appear old enough for the latter.

They worked together, fighting to stabilize Amy's condition. When Amy's heart began showing signs of irregularity, he used his radio to connect with the ED physician waiting for them at Children's Memorial. "I'm requesting a hot unload."

"Understood."

Within five minutes, thanks to a nice tailwind, the helicopter hovered, then landed with the grace of a dove. Jared barely noticed Reese's expertise, his gaze glued to the heart monitor to watch the irregular heartbeats.

"Core temp still low at thirty-two point six," Shelly informed him as they prepared to unload their young patient.

One-tenth of a degree wasn't going to cut it. Jared tucked the thermal blanket tighter around Amy as the medical team grasped the edges of the gurney lifting it from the chopper and springing the wheels so they could roll it on the ground.

They rushed Amy inside the ER, the closest trauma bay open and waiting for them. Stepping back to let the ER team take over wasn't easy, but their role in Amy's care was just about over.

He reported the medications and treatments they gave Amy to the ER doctor on staff. When he finished, he glanced at Shelly but found her attention riveted to Amy's pale face, her expression full of grave concern. He wondered what was going through her mind since they'd managed to get Amy here without any major catastrophe during the flight. Amy was looking a little more stable, less irregular heartbeats, but Shelly looked as if she'd lost her best friend.

Why did he have this insatiable need to know intimate details about Shelly? Obsessing over his flying partner, his subordinate, if he were to get technical, wasn't smart. He resented the way Shelly so easily replaced his brother's fiancée in his thoughts. Finding Leigh was more important than satisfying his curiosity about Shelly's personal life.

The ER team swarmed Amy, and within the next few minutes, the ER doc announced they had a PICU bed for her. Moments later, they wheeled Amy away.

A glance at Shelly confirmed she appeared as forlorn as he felt.

"She'll be fine," he assured her, touching her arm gently. "Our job is done here."

"I know. It's just that this is the hardest part of the job, handing the care of our patients over and walking away."

Jared silently agreed.

They returned to the chopper to find Reese waiting

patiently. "All set?" Reese asked, an unspoken question in his eyes.

Shelly nodded. "Yeah, she's doing okay. They've taken her to the pediatric ICU."

"Good to hear," Reese said with a grin. "Ready to head back?"

"You bet." Shelly climbed in first, leaving Jared to follow.

Jared knew government privacy rules prevented them from giving their pilot specific details about the patients they transported, but it felt wrong. The little girl wouldn't have gotten here without the pilot's help.

He took his seat, bumping elbows again with Shelly. The way she curled in on herself made him frown. Did she abhor his touch? Distracted by her lavender scent that reached him despite the jet fuel being so close caused him to fumble with the shoulder harness.

Listening to the sounds of Reese speaking to the tower helped calm his nerves. He didn't understand why he was so aware of Shelly, but it had to stop. There were far more important things for him to do.

Like finding Leigh Wilson and her child.

SHELLY TURNED to look out the window, telling herself it was important to keep an eye out for bird strikes. In reality, she was doing her best to ignore the tall, broad-shouldered man beside her.

After years of living in a deep freeze, her nerve endings had come leaping to life. Not for a nice guy like Reese, a man who wasn't her boss and didn't share the last name of Tyler's father. Oh no, it had to be this man beside her who created tingles of awareness rippling over her skin.

Tough beans, she told herself firmly. Get a grip. She wasn't interested, and even if she was, Ty needed stability. She'd given her unborn child a promise a long time ago. Tyler would not grow up with a series of "uncles" in his life. Every second of free time she had would be spent with him.

Her unruly hormones would just have to get over it.

There weren't any other calls over the rest of her shift, an unusually slow day when she normally preferred to be busy. At quitting time, she drove to her babysitter's house to pick up Ty. Ellen was putting toys away in the playroom when she arrived.

"How are you, big guy?" Shelly laughed when Tyler launched himself at her.

"Mommy!" His arms clamped firmly around her neck, but she didn't mind. She closed her eyes and clutched him tight, burying her face against his hair, reveling in the sweet crayon scent of childhood innocence.

She loved him so much. Tears pricked her eyelids as she thought about his upcoming medical tests. Please, please let him be okay.

"Did you fly today?" All too soon, her son wiggled in her arms, indicating he wanted down. Reluctantly, she loosened her grip and set him on his feet.

"Yep. I flew today, just once, though." Even at his young age, Ty was fascinated by her job. He claimed he could see her in the bright blue helicopter high in the sky and always waved at her as they flew over.

"Cool. I'm gonna be the pilot one day."

"You sure are," Ellen agreed as she picked up her toddler daughter Emma and took a hold of her son Alex's hand as they walked back to the kitchen. "You'll be a great pilot, Ty."

"Me, too," Alex added with a pout.

"Of course, sweetie. You, too," Ellen agreed.

"How was he today?" Shelly asked.

"Great." When Shelly narrowed her gaze, Ellen shrugged and hitched her daughter higher on her hip. "Okay, the usual. Alex and Ty had fun fighting over their toys, while Emma tried to keep up with them. The good news is that no blood was spilled and they made up."

"A good day, then." Shelly thanked her lucky stars she'd met Ellen when they'd both been in the hospital giving birth at the same time. Shelly had been fretting over child care, and Ellen had commented on how she wanted to quit her job to stay home and wouldn't mind a little extra income from babysitting. Uncertain at first, Shelly had soon met Jeff, Ellen's husband, who had wholeheartedly agreed with the idea. For five years Ellen had faithfully watched Ty, and within the last two weeks, the two kids had begun attending full-day kindergarten together. Shelly was sure the break was a welcome one for Ellen.

"Okay, Ty, say goodbye to Alex and Emma. It's time to go."

"Bye, Alex! Bye, Emma!" Tyler waved enthusiastically.

"See you tomorrow," Ellen said as they left.

"You gotta work again tomorrow?" Ty asked in dismay, wiggling as she buckled him into his child safety seat.

"Last day this week." Shelly shut the door and slid in behind the wheel. She counted herself fortunate to be able to work three twelve-hour shifts in a week, leaving four full days to spend with her son. One week, she worked day shifts and the following week, nights. Her body didn't like the night rotation, but less time away from Ty was better for him, so she embraced the schedule.

"Awww," Tyler whined.

"Don't make that long face at me." She eyed her son in

the rearview mirror. "On my days off all you want to do is go to Alex's house to play."

"'Cause Alex is my best friend," Ty announced. "We have the same birthday."

Shelly's smile dimmed, and she wondered what would happen to Ty's friendship with Alex if he was diagnosed with kidney failure.

She gave herself a mental shake, telling herself to snap out of it. She'd been in tough situations before and always found a way to manage. She'd figure it out this time, too.

Those dark days after she'd run from Boston hadn't haunted her for a long time. Fighting severe morning sickness, while trying to finish her nursing degree, while working full time to save money had caused those endless days to blur together in a fog.

Remembering that difficult time of her life ironically cheered her up. She and Ty had managed just fine. Nothing could get between them now. Especially not some stupid illness. Whatever came of Tyler's diagnostic tests, she'd deal with it.

Ellen had fed Tyler with her kids, so she spent the next hour bathing Ty, reading him a bedtime story, and putting him to bed. When the story was over, Tyler knelt at the side of his bed to say his prayers.

"God bless Mrs. Ellen, Alex, Emma, and my daddy in heaven, Amen."

Shelly smiled gently as her son bounced into bed. "Good night, Ty." She pulled the covers up and tucked them under his little pointy chin. "Sleep tight, don't let the bedbugs bite."

He giggled as he always did at the silly cliché. "Night, Mommy."

Once again, Shelly had trouble turning off her brain to

fall asleep. Her fingers itched to search the internet for more information about renal failure, but honestly, she already knew more than she wanted to.

Instead, she pulled out her journal and picked up a pen. At times like this, it helped to get her thoughts down on paper and out of her head, where they tended to whirl incessantly until she thought she'd go crazy.

Mark, I'm so worried about Ty. This single parenting stuff is hard enough without adding a serious illness to the mix. I don't think anyone other than a parent can understand how difficult this is. I've read about pediatric kidney disease, and it's all so frightening. Tyler could actually die, Mark. Our sweet little boy could die. And even if he doesn't, I can't imagine putting him through special diets, dialysis needles, and other painful procedures. He's just a little boy. He should be running and playing, not spending day upon day at the hospital.

Did you have trouble with bladder infections as a child? Did your parents? It's times like this that I really resent you leaving me alone. I want answers, no matter how unreasonable that sounds. What if he needs a kidney transplant? The thought of anything happening to our son makes me cry. I'm dripping tears on this as I write.

I've accepted the fact that we were never meant to be, even though Ty's illness has made me wonder about you and your family. I'm doing my best not to wallow in the past. Ty is my future. If you were here, I'd lean on you for support, but you're not. All I have is my internal stubbornness and determination.

Traits that I know used to drive you crazy. It's a small comfort to know they're working for me now.

Shelly.

∾

JARED IMMEDIATELY NOTICED the dark circles beneath Shelly's eyes when she entered the debriefing room the next morning. Granted, 0700 was early, but Shelly barely said good morning, before helping herself to a cup of coffee and sliding into a seat off to the side, far away from everyone.

He frowned, his instincts screaming at him that something was wrong. Late last night, he'd reviewed the notes Frank Holmes had left regarding the Lifeline employees. Shelly's file was thin, she'd been a pediatric nurse for almost four years and had been flying for the past two.

Her emergency contact was listed as Mrs. Ellen Cooley, and the relationship was friend. He assumed that meant Shelly had no husband, although he knew there could be an ex in the picture.

What had happened last night? He wished he knew Shelly well enough to ask, but he didn't. Sipping his coffee, he listened to the transport details that the team had done overnight.

As soon as the debriefing was over, Shelly disappeared. He remembered finding her in the lounge yesterday morning, her eyes closed and brackets of concern tugging at her mouth. Maybe whatever was bothering her wasn't a new thing. He moved in that direction, but his name stopped him.

"Jared? Phone call for you. Says it's important."

He glanced over his shoulder. "Okay, I'll take it in my office." Cutting through the lounge, he entered his office and picked up the phone. "Hello?"

"Jared." His mother's tearful voice flowed over the line. "Your father's heart is getting worse. The doctors say that it's only pumping at thirty percent."

A lump of concrete hardened in his gut. He closed his eyes and rubbed his forehead. He'd known his father had heart disease, he'd already gone through one open-heart procedure. But apparently his father had taken a turn for the worse.

"Did they recommend any other tests?"

"No. They said there's nothing more they can do. He's not a candidate for more surgery." His mother's voice broke, and she began to sob. "Oh, Jared, what am I going to do?"

"Please, Mom, don't cry." Yet Jared couldn't blame her, his throat tightened, and a throbbing headache settled behind his eyes. He forced himself to sound calm. "Dad may not be able to have surgery, but his condition isn't hopeless, yet. Lots of people live with only thirty percent ejection fraction."

He could hear his mother struggling to get herself under control. "I know, I'm sorry. I'm just so worried. I wish you could come home, Jared, at least for a few days. Please?"

Familiar guilt slammed into him. He swallowed hard. "I've only been here a few days, but I'll see what I can do. Tell Dad I'll call him later. I'll call his doctor, too."

His mother blew her nose on the other end of the connection. "I understand. I know your work is important."

Jared sighed and rubbed his temple. "It's not just work, Mom. I told you I'm trying to find her."

He didn't have to explain further, his mother knew exactly who he was searching for. "Oh, Jared. Do you think it's possible? After all these years?"

"I don't know. The PI confirmed Leigh's family lived here in Milwaukee and that she was last seen here. I plan to pick up the investigation where he left off. That idiot PI didn't care as much about finding Leigh as I do." Jared scowled, ticked that the PI had continued to take his father's money despite making absolutely no progress on the case. From what he could tell, the guy had done nothing for the past two years.

Two years out of six wasted on that jerk.

His mother's voice brightened. "Well, then. You'll call us when you have news?"

"I promise. Now try to stay strong. Dad needs you."

His mother promised, then disconnected from the call. He dropped his head in his hands, overwhelmed by a feeling of hopelessness. He knew his father's health wasn't good, but this latest news brought a new sense of urgency.

He needed to find Leigh Wilson and her child soon. His dad deserved to see his only grandchild in the short time he had left.

"Jared?" A familiar husky female voice interrupted his thoughts. A soft hand dropped onto his shoulder, squeezing gently. "Are you okay?"

He lifted his head, surprised to see Shelly standing there, looking at him with concern. Her small hand radiated warmth through the fabric of his flight suit, and he reached up to cover it with his.

"Not really." He surprised himself by blurting the truth. "I just got a call from home about my dad's heart failure. According to my mom, there isn't anything more they can do for him."

"I'm sorry." Shelly didn't pull away from his touch, and his pulse skipped with awareness. "Maybe you should take a few days off and fly home."

Jared almost laughed at her words, an echo of his mother's. The light pressure of her hand grounded him. He brushed his thumb over the satiny smoothness of her hand. "Thanks, but it's not that bad, at least, not yet."

"Maybe not, but it can't be easy for you to be here, so

many miles away." She subtly slipped her hand from his, and he instantly regretted the loss.

He tilted his head to look at her. "You sound as if you're speaking from experience."

Her expression clouded, and she took a step back. "Possibly, but I won't know for sure until the diagnostic tests have been done."

"Your parents?" Jared couldn't help prying for information. At least this explained her apparent lack of sleep.

"No, my parents are dead." Her expression closed, and Jared battled a wave of frustration. He wanted to offer his support, but she seemed determined to keep distance between them.

"I'm sorry to hear that." Who were the important people in her life? Other than her friend, Mrs. Ellen Cooley?

"It's okay, it happened a few years ago." Shelly shrugged and cleared her throat. "I came to let you know I'm heading over to Children's Memorial to do a follow up on Amy. The hospital is just across the street, and I have my pager in case we get a flight call."

He wanted to join her, but she hadn't offered and he felt awkward inviting himself along. Besides, he couldn't waste any more time. He needed to find Leigh Wilson and fast. "Go ahead. Let me know how Amy and her parents are doing."

"I will." She gave him a curious look, and he belatedly realized she may have expected him to come along. In an instant, the expression was gone and she turned to leave.

Against his will, his gaze clung to her curvy figure, flatteringly displayed in her flight suit. Pulling himself together, he did his best to ignore the emptiness of his office after Shelly left.

He didn't understand what was wrong with him. He'd

met plenty of beautiful women, but none had captured his interest the way Shelly had. He pulled out his list of restaurants and nightclubs to call regarding any former employees named Leigh Wilson.

But despite his best intentions, his thoughts continued to return to Shelly. She was a toucher, a nurturer. He liked being the recipient of her caring a little too much. Especially when he knew she had troubles of her own, a weight that she carried across her shoulders. She deserved to have someone share the burden.

As soon as the thought entered his mind, he shoved it away. The mere image of another man offering comfort and support to Shelly depressed him more than the possibility of never finding his brother's fiancée and child.

3

J ared worked on reviewing Lifeline's financial statements until another call came in. He read the display on the pager, then called dispatch for more information.

"A semitruck jackknifed into multiple motor vehicles on the interstate. At least one family with kids involved," the dispatcher told him.

"Flight conditions?"

"Rain has stopped for the moment; you're good to go. One Lifeline crew is already on scene."

"Got it." Jared hung up the phone and headed outside to the hangar.

Shelly was already there, once again talking to Reese. Even as he watched, Shelly gave the pilot's arm a quick squeeze, before stepping away. Jared frowned. Maybe there was something going on between Shelly and the pilot after all?

"Ready?" He couldn't help the sharp bite to his tone.

Shelly glanced up in surprise. "Of course."

Reese took his cue and gave them a quick rundown of

the location and flight plan. Within minutes, they were airborne.

Jared wanted to ask Shelly how Amy was doing but forced himself to stay quiet. Reese was keeping in contact with the base and getting information on where they could land. Through the chopper's window, Jared could see swarms of paramedics and firefighters amidst the smoke rising from the crash scene. The first Lifeline helicopter was still there, too. For a moment, he was strongly reminded of the night his brother had died.

Shaking off the unwelcome memories, he followed Shelly out of the helicopter the moment Reese landed. They were instantly flagged down by one of the paramedics.

"There are three kids trapped in the green van," he said, waving a hand at the crushed vehicle. "We're still trying to get them out."

"Any kids in the other wrecks?" Jared asked, unable to tear his gaze from the destruction. There were crushed and mangled cars everywhere, tossed around as if they were mini toy cars dropped by a child.

"No, thankfully. But we have one dead victim, the driver of the first car the truck hit. The van was the second vehicle hit by the trailer, and the kids' parents are in bad shape."

As the paramedic spoke, Jared saw a badly bruised and battered man lying on a stretcher, his neck covered in a C-collar. He was being wheeled to the first helicopter. Mark? He took a hesitant step forward, then abruptly pulled himself together.

No. Not Mark. His brother was dead. Just like the driver of the first car was dead. He shook his head to dislodge the painful memories. Why were they suddenly haunting him now? Because of his father's decline and his renewed promise to find Leigh? He blinked and realized Shelly had already dashed over to the green van. There were kids inside that needed him. He quickly followed.

Shelly crouched beside the firefighters who had already sawn off the door. Then she crawled inside through the small opening.

"What are you doing?" Panic surged, and he rushed forward to grab her arm, preventing her from going further.

She shot him an incredulous look over her shoulder. "Those kids are scared and crying. I'm the smallest one here, therefore the most logical person to get them out."

He didn't like it, didn't like the potential danger. But if the situation had been reversed, he would have done the same thing. And technically, flight staff were considered first responders. From inside the van, he heard the muffled sounds of crying. At least that much was a good sign. Complete silence would have been much worse.

"Okay, I'll see what else we can do to help." Jared let go of Shelly's arm. She wiggled through the space and disappeared inside the van. He turned to the firefighter still working on enlarging the opening with the saw.

"Need a hand?" He waited until the guy took another chunk of metal out of the van.

"Nah, I have it."

Helpless, Jared couldn't do anything else but watch. And wait. He remembered the twisted metal wreck that had been Mark's car after the accident. Had the first responders worked like this to get him out? Had they known it was already too late? That Mark had died on impact?

"There, that should be large enough to do it."

Jared realized the firefighter was talking to him. *Come on, man, focus,* he lectured himself. *Mark is gone. Those kids need you to rub a few brain cells together and think.*

"Yes, it works." He climbed partially inside the van.

There wasn't enough room to get all the way in with Shelly and the kids already inside.

As his eyes adjusted to the dim interior, he could see Shelly was wedged between the seats, trying to free the kids. "How are they?"

"Not bad. Thankfully, they're all in car seats and booster seats. I'm freeing up the smallest one now. Get ready, I'll hand her over to you."

Jared didn't know how Shelly could move, much less wiggle around enough to free the smallest child's car seat from the back. The little girl looked to be about two years old. There was some blood on the girl's head where she was cut, but her lungs worked well enough. She bellowed louder as Shelly handed her car seat over.

"Shh, it's okay, I have you." Jared held the car seat close as he backed out of the van. "You're going to be fine." He set the car seat on the gurney, hoping that being out of the car would calm her down.

It didn't.

Her crying meant that he couldn't hear much as he listened to her heart and lungs. After a quick neuro exam and a brief physical exam, he let out a soundless sigh of relief. The girl must have been nicely cushioned by the car seat because, other than the cut on her forehead, she appeared to be fine.

He turned to the firefighter. "Where are the parents?"

"Already on their way to Trinity Medical Center." The firefighter nodded toward the first helicopter that was lifting off from the scene. "They were both unconscious and badly injured. Took the brunt of the crash."

"I hope they make it," he said, more to himself than to the firefighter. "One of you needs to hang on to this cutie for me, she needs to stay in the car seat until we get her to the ER."

"I'll take her."

Jared handed the girl over to the paramedic. "Tape the cut on her forehead with butterfly tape."

"Jared?" Shelly's voice called him from deep inside the van.

"Yeah?" He crawled back through the opening. "What is it?"

"There are twin boys back here, and one of them has a broken arm. They were belted in booster seats on either side of the car seat. I'm worried about possible neck injuries. Grab a couple of C-collars and a longboard."

"Got it." Jared shimmied back out and grabbed the pediatric longboard from beneath the gurney mattress, then set two small C-collars on top. The board would only fit so far through the opening. "Can you reach it?"

Shelly didn't answer, but Jared could see her forehead wrinkled in concentration as she unstrapped one twin and fitted the C-collar into place. The boy, whom he estimated to be five or six, didn't like the restriction and started to cry. Shelly talked to him soothingly and kept his spine in alignment as much as possible when sliding him onto the board. Jared reached in to help stabilize.

"I have him." Jared summoned a reassuring smile. "Hey there, big guy. I bet you're hurting, aren't you? Well, we're going to fix you right up. Now hold very still so we can get you out of here, okay?" He eased the child down the board, then strapped him on. Backing out of the van, he pulled the longboard out with the firefighter's help.

They set the boy on the gurney as the little girl was still being held in her car seat by a paramedic. He slid the longboard out from beneath the child so they could use it on the other twin. Jared saw that Shelly was right. The boy's left arm was broken. He was also covered in minor cuts and bruises. Internal bleeding? Possibly, but he really hoped not.

"What's your name?" Jared tried to distract the boy as he started an IV.

"K-Kevin." He answered the question between hiccupping sobs.

"What's your brother's name? And your sister's?" Jared kept up a steady stream of questions.

"Kyle is my b-brother. K-immy is the baby." Once Jared had given Kevin a very small dose of pain medication, the child settled down enough so Jared could splint his arm. Kevin would need to be taken to Children's Memorial as soon as possible.

Shelly emerged with Kyle who didn't appear to have broken bones but cried whenever anyone touched his foot. Between them, they discussed with Reese the possibility of transporting both kids at the same time.

"We can make it work," Reese assured them.

"What about their sister?" Shelly asked. "We can't leave her here, not when her parents are at the hospital as well."

Jared signaled for the paramedic holding Kimmy to come over. "Can you bring her to Children's Memorial?"

"Wait." Shelly's face betrayed her distress. "Reese, what if the paramedic sat up front with Kimmy on his lap? Would the additional personnel impact the weight limit? She's a peanut, and the car seat isn't much more."

"How much do you weigh?" Reese asked.

"One eighty-five."

Reese considered it for a moment, then nodded. "We can do it. Let's keep the kids together."

"Thank you," Shelly said.

He and Shelly hefted the twin boys and their respective

gurneys on board. It was a tight fit. Normally the chopper was designed for one patient at a time, but since these patients were just little kids, he was determined to make it work.

"It's a short ride," Shelly pointed out as if reading his mind.

He nodded and donned his helmet. They could only talk to the boys one at a time through their communication devices, but it didn't matter since they were landing on the rooftop helipad of Children's Memorial in less than fifteen minutes.

They hadn't called for a hot unload because the kids were stable, but the news of their arrival with three kids had already reached the emergency department. Several staff members were waiting for them when they jumped down from the helicopter.

"Let's get these kids inside," the ER physician took Kevin, the more seriously injured of the two under his wing.

"Have you notified social services?" Shelly asked.

Jared knew what she was getting at. With the kids' parents' condition so tenuous, they would need to find extended family to take care of the little ones, and soon.

"Yeah, they're on it."

Within the hour, they had the boys checked out, confirming Kevin did have some internal bleeding to go along with his broken arm, resulting in a quick trip to the OR. Kyle had a broken foot, but no other injuries. Kimmy was the least injured of the three.

As they were getting ready to leave, he noticed Shelly's gaze lingered on the kids as she reluctantly followed him out.

"Are you okay?" He held the elevator door open that would take them back up to the roof.

"Fine."

He didn't believe her. Maybe he wasn't the only one with ghosts haunting him. "You did an amazing job back there, getting those kids out of the wreck." He couldn't help but admire her ability to connect with kids. Maybe he should be envious about her possible relationship with the pilot. She certainly deserved to have a family of her own.

And he wasn't interested in going down that path. Not now, not when he had a missing woman and child to find.

"No braver than anyone else," she contradicted. "Those firefighters are probably still out there. We have the easy job, get the victims out and bring them in. Those guys will be clearing the scene for hours yet."

"Maybe so, but we have the responsibility of making life and death decisions."

"They do, too."

"All set?" Reese asked as they walked out onto the helipad.

"Yeah." He tried not to notice the way Reese looked at Shelly. "The three kids should be fine, but I'm wondering how the parents are doing."

"I can't bear the thought of those kids being orphaned . . ." Shelly's voice trailed off.

Jared rested the palm of his hand on her back. "I'm sure they'll find other family members to take them in."

Her gaze furrowed. "But what if they don't have other family?"

"They will." He spoke with confidence, hating to see her so distraught. "Those little kids will win anyone's heart."

Shelly just stared at him for a long minute, then grabbed her helmet and plunked it on her head, preventing further conversation.

But Jared sensed her thoughts remained troubled as Reese flew them back to the chopper base.

THOSE KIDS WOULD WIN anyone's heart. Jared's words reverberated over and over in her head. Despite her efforts to remain professional, she couldn't help but compare the three kids' situation with her son's.

If she were suddenly injured, who would take care of Tyler? Oh, sure, Ellen would step in to help out, as would Kate or Reese, but long-term? Who would adopt him? How would anyone know who Ty's father was, to find his family? She didn't have any siblings and hadn't told anyone the truth about her past.

The idea of Ty being left alone in the world troubled her for the remainder of her shift. Maybe she needed to do something, like leave some sort of will requesting Mark's family be contacted if anything happened to her.

The idea didn't sit well, but it was better than doing nothing or leaving the decision regarding Ty's care to complete strangers. She glanced at her watch for the third time in ten minutes. Still an hour to go before she was off duty. Jared must have noticed her antsy behavior because he crossed over to sit beside her.

"Hungry? We can get something to eat at the hospital café across the street," he offered. "It's close enough that we can still respond if there's a call."

Flabbergasted, she stared at him for a moment. "Oh, no thanks. I, uh, want to get out of here on time. I need to get home."

Jared frowned. "Do you need to leave early?"

She wanted to do exactly that, but that would mean

asking the night shift nurse to come in an hour early. "No, I can wait for Christine to come in."

"There's a paramedic here that can cover for you," Jared said softly. "The minimum flight crew for peds is a physician and nurse or paramedic. Go on home, you look exhausted."

Hesitating, she inwardly debated. Jared was right about the minimum flight crew requirement, but she took her responsibilities seriously. Leaving before the end of her shift didn't seem right. But the desire to see her son was strong, so she nodded.

"Thanks, Jared." She hurried to grab her stuff out of her locker. Back in the lounge, Jared seemed to be waiting.

He caught her arm as she brushed past. "Shelly?"

She stopped swinging around to face him. "What is it? Change your mind?"

His eyes were so close, so amazingly blue. Almost against her will, she moved a step closer. His hand cupping her elbow was strong yet gentle.

"No. I—nothing." His hand slid up her arm to her shoulder, his fingers tucking a strand of her hair behind her ear. "If you need something, let me know. I can help."

His feather-light touch sent her pulse skipping into triple digits. Her eyes widened in surprise when he took another step closer.

Her breath tangled in her throat, and she caught herself mesmerized by his intense gaze.

Shocked at the unwelcome attraction, she took a step back, breaking the intangible connection between them. "I . . . don't need any help. But thanks for the offer."

"Anytime." Was that disappointment she saw in his gaze?

Shaking her head at her foolishness, she left the hangar. Outside, she released her pent-up breath in a rush. What in the world was wrong with her? She didn't gaze longingly into the eyes of a man. Especially not one she worked with.

Jared was her boss for heaven's sake!

Disappointed in herself, she hopped into her car and headed toward home, stopping at a small gas station long enough to grab something to eat. She knew Ellen would have already fed Ty, so she tucked the sandwich away for later.

She was forty-five minutes early picking up Ty, but Ellen didn't mind. Shelly took Tyler home and made an effort to spend some quality time with her son. Emma's birthday was coming up, so she helped him painstakingly color a birthday card for her. After he'd finished, she ran him a bath before tucking him into bed.

Eating her sandwich with one hand, she surfed the internet with the other, seeking an online will. When she found the one she liked, she hit the print button. It didn't take long to fill out the information. She needed to have it witnessed but felt better after taking action to make sure Mark's family would be notified if anything happened to her.

Halfway through her sandwich, she realized it tasted awful and tossed the rest of it out. She downed some milk, hoping to kill the aftertaste.

Still restless, she picked up her journal again. Normally she didn't write in it every night, but there was nothing normal about Tyler's situation.

And a one-sided conversation was probably healthier than none.

Mark, I wrote out a will today. Do you have any idea how hard it was for me to put in writing the directive to place Ty in the hands of your family? I never thought of things like this in those early days, after I ran from your parents. But today I was once again reminded how fragile life is. I pray I remain healthy for many years to come.

Your parents were so awful to me the day I showed up to tell them I was pregnant. Of course, it was also the day of your funeral, so I understand they were grieving. But your mother scared me, shrieking about you and offering me a million dollars to leave my baby with her. Money! She actually offered me money to give up my child. What kind of woman is she? How can I leave Tyler with someone like that?

Yet my alternative is to leave him with strangers. Talk about a no-win situation. I shudder to think of what living with your parents would do to our son. I want to believe they'd love and care for Ty, but I also know how much you complained about how they pushed you to become an attorney when you weren't at all interested in the law. I'm still surprised you dropped out of school without telling them. Still, look at how many years you bent to their will. I won't have Ty molded into some image they've created for him.

Our son has dreams of his own. Ty wants to be a pilot, and I'll do anything to help him realize his dreams.

Shelly

SHE SET HER JOURNAL ASIDE, thinking about Mark's family as she crawled into bed. Yet somehow, right before she fell asleep, she realized her thoughts had drifted to Jared.

Fiery, stabbing stomach pains woke her in the early morning hours. Hugging herself around the waist, she dragged herself to the bathroom in the nick of time, losing the contents of her stomach in one horrible heave.

Shaking, she slid to the floor.

Her muscles morphed into rubber bands, weak and quivering. The cramping pain in her stomach hit again, and she hung over the commode, gagging as her body seemed intent on getting rid of everything inside her. Sweaty, she sat on the bathroom floor, feeling both hot and cold at the same time.

She tried to stand, but her legs wouldn't support her weight. Her stomach cramps continued. Pain knifed through her belly. What was wrong with her? Why did it hurt so bad?

The minutes merged into hours, and she still couldn't find the strength to crawl out of the bathroom. Worry pushed through the agony in her stomach. Something wasn't right.

She needed her phone. Ty shouldn't see her like this. With a Herculean effort, she pushed herself up but then collapsed again.

"Mommy? What's wrong?"

She lifted her head, hoping to hide the intense pain that was much worse than when she'd given birth. Ty's features blurred as she tried to focus on her son. "I'm a little sick, honey. Bring me the phone, please? I'll call for help."

As soon as Ty left, she lowered her head against the cool ceramic of the commode. She didn't have the strength of a flea. Rivulets of sweat rolled down her back. Deep in her heart, she knew there was something seriously wrong with her. More than a flu bug, that was for sure.

Maybe a ruptured appendix?

She hugged the toilet again, her stomach convulsing. She felt so awful. Had writing up her will, appointing Mark's family as legal guardians over Ty been some sort of premonition?

Was she going to die?

No! She refused to leave her son.

Ty brought her mobile phone, and it took all her strength and coordination to dial Kate at Lifeline.

"Hello?" a deep voice answered.

There was a loud buzzing in her ears. She couldn't place the voice on the other end of the line. She forced herself to concentrate. "Kate. I need to talk to Kate."

"Kate's out on a flight. Shelly? Is that you?"

Jared. She closed her eyes against another searing pain. He was the last person she wanted to talk to, but if Kate was on a flight, she didn't have a choice. Who else was working today? She didn't have a clue.

"Yes. It's me. I'm sick."

"What do you need?" The concern in Jared's tone filled her with relief.

"Something's really wrong. I think I need to go to the hospital, but I need—" She stopped abruptly as another cramping pain stole her breath.

She hadn't called 911 because she needed someone to take Tyler. That's what she was trying to explain. But the buzzing was back in her ears, drowning out the sound of Ty's concerned chatter. The phone slipped from her grasp, clattering to the floor.

Until, at last, there was blessed silence.

4

J ared hung up the phone, his instincts screaming that Shelly needed help. *Now.* He leaped to his feet, heading straight for his office. Shelly's address was in her file.

He was most familiar with the area right around the hangar, and thankfully she didn't live that far away. Clutching her address in hand, he rushed from his office.

Ivan Ames, one of their pediatric paramedics, glanced up in surprise when Jared dashed through the lounge.

"Where's the fire?" Ivan asked.

He ignored him. "Call Dr. Simmons to cover for me. Shelly's in trouble." He didn't so much as glance back as he exited the building.

How he managed to find Shelly's house without any difficulty, he had no idea. The small, cozy ranch-style home was exactly the sort of place he'd have expected Shelly to live. Better than his fancy condo any day.

He threw the gearshift into park and slid out of the car. He ran up the driveway, lifted his fist, and pounded on the door.

"Shelly! Are you in there? Open up!" He tried the door handle, but it was locked. Was she too weak to answer? He pounded again, then stepped back, surveying the house to estimate which window would be the easiest to break.

The door abruptly opened, but there wasn't anyone there. His gaze dropped. A small boy with sandy brown hair and big brown eyes, about the same age as the twins they'd rescued the previous day, stood behind the screen door.

"My mommy is sick. Are you the nine one one she called?" The boy's lower lip quivered as if he were about to burst into tears.

Mommy? His gut clenched in shock; he didn't know Shelly had a son. Still, he didn't waste time pondering the news or wondering where his father might be. He dropped to one knee so he was eye level with the boy, then spoke reassuringly through the screen. "Yes, I know your mom is sick. I'm Jared, a friend of your mom's. I'm a doctor, so she called me for help. Will you let me in?"

The boy regarded him soberly for a long moment, then nodded. He reached up, standing on tiptoe to unlock the screen door. Thank heavens, Jared thought as he opened the door. The boy was right to be wary of strangers—the last thing he wanted to do was to scare Shelly's son.

"Where's your mom?"

"In the bathroom." The boy stuck his fingers in his mouth as he ran through the small living room, pointing to the first door in the short hallway.

If he hadn't been staring at the floor, he might have stepped on her head. She was sprawled facedown on the linoleum, dressed in an oversize sleepshirt, as if she'd tried to crawl from the bathroom but hadn't had the strength.

Jared's breath lodged in his throat. With an effort, he shoved his personal feelings aside and surveyed her as a physician. He knelt beside her, feeling for a pulse. The thready beat was present, but not as strong as he'd like. She was breathing, but definitely weak. Gently he shook her. "Shelly? It's Jared. Can you hear me?"

She didn't move. Conscious of little ears hovering beside him, Jared swallowed a frustrated sigh. Where was the phone? He should have called 911 right away but had wanted to see what was going on for himself first.

But it was worse than what he'd expected. She needed help, fast.

"Is my mommy okay?"

Jared paused in the act of picking up her mobile phone from the floor of her outstretched hand. If he called the paramedics, loud sirens and bright flashing lights from the ambulance and accompanying police cars would no doubt frighten Shelly's son.

He took a deep breath and reassessed the situation. She was alive, breathing on her own, and had a pulse. No reason to panic. "We're going to take your mom to the hospital, okay? I'd like another doctor to check her out."

"'Cause you don't know what to do?" the boy asked with a frown.

That made him smile. "No, because I need more supplies. Is that okay with you?"

The brown-haired boy nodded, but his eyes remained wide with apprehension. Jared wished he could say something to reassure him. He knelt beside her, gently rolled her over, then lifted Shelly into his arms.

She didn't weigh much, but the mechanics of getting her off the floor while trying to stand wasn't easy. He had to lean against the wall as support. In the living room, he laid her on the sofa, then turned back to the boy.

"What's your name?"

"Ty." The boy watched him warily. He wore thin Avenger pajamas, but his feet were bare.

"Okay, Ty. I need you to find your shoes and socks. Can you do that for me?"

The boy scampered off as if worried Jared would leave without him. Jared took a moment to examine Shelly's pupils, letting his breath out in relief when they were both equal and reactive to light.

What in the world had happened to her? Was she sick? Did she have some disease like diabetes that he wasn't aware of?

"Ready?" Ty returned sounding almost cheerful.

"Let's go." Jared lifted Shelly off the sofa. "Open the door for me, Ty."

Shelly's son was a trouper, helping in every way that he could. Jared laid Shelly's limp form along the back seat of his car. When he eased out, he found Ty standing there, watching him. Luckily, the autumn day was warm enough that he wouldn't need to waste time searching for Ty's coat.

"Here, you can get up front with me," he instructed the child.

"Uh-uh. I'm supposed to sit in the back, with my booster seat."

Jared rubbed a hand over his eyes. As a pediatric specialist he knew the rules, but he didn't want to waste any more time.

"Ty, we have to hurry. I promise to drive safely; the hospital is just a few blocks away."

The boy eyed him uncertainly but obliged him by climbing into the front passenger seat. Figuring any seat belt was better than nothing, he quickly buckled him in.

By the time they arrived at the hospital, Shelly was starting to moan. Grateful she was beginning to wake up,

Jared pulled right up to the ambulance bay at Trinity Medical Center's Emergency Department.

"I need help! Bring a gurney!"

Two nurses rushed outside, wheeling a hospital gurney between them, then helped him get her onto it.

"What happened?" one of them asked.

"I don't know. Shelly Bennett is a nurse at Lifeline. She called for help, said she was sick. I think she's been throwing up in the bathroom. When I found her, she was unconscious on the bathroom floor but had a pulse and was breathing." Hating to feel helpless, Jared racked his brain for anything that might help. "I'll fill out the initial information, then head over to Lifeline. I might be able to find more in her file."

"Knowing her past medical history would be nice," one of the nurses observed dryly. "But don't bother with Lifeline, hopefully she gets her medical care here. If so, we'll have everything we need in her medical record."

"Yeah, okay . . ." They quickly whisked Shelly away.

He stared after her, wishing he could do more. A little hand snuck into his, and Jared glanced down in surprise. For a brief moment, he'd completely forgotten Shelly's son. The kid looked so forlorn, he instinctively reached down and lifted the boy into his arms.

"Hey there. Guess what? Those nice people are going to take care of your mom. How about if we hang out together for a while?"

Ty's lower lip trembled, and he held himself stiff in Jared's arms. "I wanna see my mom."

Jared's heart squeezed in sympathy. The poor kid didn't even know him. Who were the familiar people in his life? Where was his father? Jared had no idea. But he couldn't abandon this little boy, so he forced a smile.

"I know you do," he said soothingly. "I promise you'll get to see her soon."

Big fat tears slid down Ty's cheeks. For a moment, the boy reminded him of his younger brother, Mark. Five years his junior, Mark had been about the same age when their dog had died. Ty's tear-streaked face looked achingly familiar. But, unlike Mark, he didn't wail or cry. Instead, Ty simply laid his head on Jared's shoulder, snaking his small, sturdy arms up until they were wrapped tightly around Jared's neck.

He held the boy close, smoothed a hand over his back, longing to reassure him. The irony of the situation wasn't lost on him. Amazing how Ty was about the same age as his missing niece or nephew. Jared shoved aside the longing. He couldn't worry about Leigh Wilson or her child right now. Ty needed him. But he was as helpless now as he'd been twenty-two years ago in comforting Mark after losing their pet. Until he knew exactly what was wrong with Shelly, there wasn't much he could say or do. Except keep Shelly's son company.

He'd promised the boy he could see his mother. So they'd wait for however long it took.

He wanted to believe he'd keep his promise. That Shelly would be fine and Ty would soon get to see his mom.

WAITING WAS PURE AGONY. How did families stand it? He might be a doctor, but there was certainly something wrong with the way the medical system worked. Jared and Ty had been waiting over an hour for word on Shelly's condition.

And they'd heard nothing.

Jared thrust his fingers through his hair in exasperation.

What in the world was taking them so long? He deduced they were performing a wide barrage of tests to figure out what was wrong. Still, the basic lab results should be back by now.

"I'm hungry," Ty announced. For being so young, Ty had been incredibly patient. "And I hafta go to the bathroom."

He glanced at his watch for the fifth time in as many minutes, stifling a sigh. "Let me tell the nurses where we're going so they can find us when your mom is ready for visitors."

Jared quickly found the triage nurse, watching from the corner of his eye as Ty hopped from one foot to the other. Apparently, the kid wasn't kidding about needing to go. "We need to take a break. Here's my pager number—please page me as soon as you have some information."

"I will, Dr. O'Connor." The nurse flashed a distracted smile. "We should hear something soon."

"Not soon enough," he muttered. Spinning on his heel, he returned to Ty and reached for the boy's hand. "Let's go."

Who would have thought that a trip to the men's room would take so long? Ty immediately crossed over to the urinal on the wall, asking about it. Hadn't the boy been in a men's room before? Inside the stall, Ty locked and unlocked the door several times. After using the facilities, he stretched up over the counter to wash his hands, then played with the auto-dryer machine until Jared put a stop to it.

"Your hands are dry enough. I thought you were hungry?" Jared raised his voice to carry over the roar of the dryer.

"I am." Ty nodded enthusiastically, pulling out of Jared's grasp to shove his hands back under the hot air.

"Let's go to the cafeteria, then." Jared held the door

open, gesturing for Ty to leave. "We have to hurry or we might miss breakfast. What are you in the mood for?"

"Hotcakes and sausage." Ty finally abandoned the novelty of the men's room and skipped down the hall to the elevator. "Mom loves hotcakes and sausage."

Really? Jared hid a smile. Shelly may like sausage, but he could also see her cooking Ty's favorite meal for him as if it were. He suspected she was a great mother. With a frown, he realized Ty was still wearing his Avenger pajamas. Guess he wouldn't be nearly as good a father considering he hadn't even dressed the kid. At least Ty didn't seem to mind.

As Jared ate his hotcakes and sausage, the same meal he'd ordered for Ty, he tried to think of a subtle way to broach the subject of Ty's absent father. His pager went off. He read the ED number in relief. Finally, some news.

"Stay here a minute, Ty. I need to use the phone over there." He indicated a hospital house phone mounted on the wall a few tables from where they were seated.

"Okay." Ty shoved a huge bite of pancake into his mouth, syrup dribbling on his chin.

Jared strode over to the phone. He dialed the number on his pager and waited for someone to pick up. "This is Dr. O'Connor," he identified himself. "Did someone page about Shelly Bennett?"

"Yes, this is Erica, the nurse caring for Shelly. She's awake. Do you have her son, Tyler, with you?"

"We're in the cafeteria eating breakfast right now. Shelly's awake? What did her lab tests show?"

"So far we've ruled out a hot appendix and gallstones. She was severely dehydrated, so we gave her a couple liters of fluid. She's weak and still extremely nauseated. We're still working her up to find the source of her pain."

Jared frowned and rubbed his jaw. He'd thought for sure she had appendicitis. "What was her glucose?"

"On the low side of normal. We have her medical information; she's not diabetic. Anyway, will you bring her son up to see her? She's very agitated and asking about him. I think she'll relax when she sees for herself that he's all right."

"Of course. He's almost finished with his breakfast." He glanced back at the table, but Ty's small brown head wasn't anywhere in sight. The blood drained from his face, and he quickly slammed the phone down.

Where was Ty? Frantic, his gaze searched the nearby tables. Good grief, he'd only been away for three minutes. How could the boy have disappeared that fast?

"Ty?" Jared wove between the cafeteria tables, bumping into chairs. "*Tyler!*"

"What?" Ty's small head suddenly popped out from underneath the table. Jared's breath left his lungs in a whoosh.

The boy was safe.

"Don't do that to me." His hands were shaking as he reached out to pull the boy close. He was flunking fatherhood 101. He'd almost lost Shelly's son.

"Do what?" Puzzled, Tyler cocked his head and pulled back. "I dropped my fork, see?"

Belatedly, Jared noticed the fork clutched in the boy's hand. By dropping his fork, the kid had nearly shocked Jared's heart straight into asystole. Straight-line all the way.

"I was scared when I couldn't see you—never mind. Are you almost finished? Your mom is ready for visitors."

Tyler's eyes widened with anticipation, and he eagerly abandoned his plate, the fork clattering to the table. "I'm all done."

"Me, too." Jared grinned. "Let's go see your mom."

SHELLY SHIFTED on the uncomfortable gurney mattress, blinking at the brightness of the overhead lights. Everything was fuzzy, confusing since the moment she'd awoken on the wrong side of a hospital bed. If her stomach didn't hurt so much, she'd chalk the whole thing up to a bad dream.

But the pain was real. So was the nausea. Through her lashes, she could see an IV bag dripping fluid into a vein in her arm. Who had brought her here? And, most importantly, where was her son? She'd asked the nurse where Tyler was, and she kept saying he'd be there soon. But how could that be? Had she somehow left him home alone?

The thought of Ty had her struggling against the weakness, pulling herself upright on the gurney with supreme effort.

"Whoa, there, where do you think you're going?" The nurse—Shelly thought her name was Erica—ran to her side and placed a hand on her shoulder to prevent her from sitting up too far. "Just take it easy and lie down. You're not going anywhere yet."

"Let me out of here. I need to find my son. He's only five, do you understand that? I have to find him!" Shelly knew she sounded hysterical but couldn't help it. How had she gotten out of her home and to the hospital? An ambulance? Had the paramedics left Ty home alone? Maybe he'd been sleeping in his bed and they'd missed him. Or he may have hidden from them in fear. Dear Lord, she had to find him. She shoved the nurse out of her way. She'd crawl out of there on her belly if necessary.

"Shh, I told you, your son will be here soon. He's with Dr. O'Connor. They're on their way from the cafeteria now."

Dr. O'Connor? Exhausted by her efforts, Shelly dropped back on the gurney and closed her eyes. Why was Ty with a doctor? Had she collapsed at the hospital during Ty's kidney testing?

"Shelly?"

Dazed, she squinted against the lights. A familiar blond-haired man stood at her bedside. The name finally sank into her shriveled brain. Dr. O'Connor was Jared. Slowly, pieces of the morning's events came back to her. She'd called Lifeline for help. Jared had answered.

Jared had her son.

"Ty." Shelly focused her gaze on her son holding Jared's hand, standing beside him. Her throat swelled in relief. He was safe. Thankfully, he was safe. "Are you all right?"

Ty nodded, and Jared urged him farther into the room. Ty grabbed the side rail, apparently willing to climb aboard, until Jared intercepted him.

"Hang on, I'll pull this down for you."

Jared lowered the railing. Shelly reached over and wrapped her arm around her son, lowering her head until she could lay her cheek against his silky fine hair.

Tyler was fine. Still wearing his Avenger pajamas, sticky with a substance that smelled an awful lot like maple syrup, but otherwise fine. Better than fine.

"I'm so sorry, Ty. I didn't mean to get sick."

"Are you coming home soon?" Ty asked.

"I don't think she's ready to go home just yet," Jared interjected.

"Yes, I'm coming home soon. I only need to rest." Shelly didn't hesitate to override Jared's objections. She let go of Ty and relaxed back against the gurney mattress, sucking in a harsh breath when her stomach cramped again. The ER doc had reassured her that her appendix was fine. But, man, her stomach hurt. If this was just a bad case of the flu, she'd go home for sure. She needed a bathroom, and no way was she using a bedpan.

Uh-uh. No way, no how.

"Erica? I think Shelly needs help," Jared called out to the nurse seated at the desk not far from Shelly's cubicle.

The nurse hurried back. "What can I get you?"

"You can get me out of here," she said firmly. "I need to go home. Where's the doctor?" She wasn't in the mood to be poked and prodded. Why didn't they just let her rest in peace?

"Relax, I have some good news. We found the source of your problem. Seems you have food poisoning in the form of an intestinal staph infection."

"Staph? From what?" Shelly wrinkled her forehead in confusion as she thought back to what she'd eaten after Ty had gone to bed. "The sandwich."

Erica leaned closer, her gaze intent. "What sandwich?"

"My dinner last night. I bought a sandwich at the local gas station. I only ate half of it because it tasted awful. I threw the rest of it away."

"Ah, that's probably it." Erica smiled.

Shelly felt like a fool. Ending up in the emergency department of Trinity Medical Center just because of a lousy turkey and mayo sandwich. How humiliating.

"Well, at least that's one mystery solved," Erica was saying. "We're starting you on IV antibiotics."

She pulled herself together. "Good. Give me the first dose, then I'm out of here." She knew she was being stubbornly persistent, but she didn't care.

"Not without twenty-four hours' worth of IV antibiotics, you're not." Erica's expression grew strained.

Shelly knew she wasn't being a very cooperative patient, but then again, that wasn't unusual. Doctors and nurses always made the worst patients. She didn't care if she was only adding to the cliché. She steeled her resolve.

Ty needed her at home.

"I'll go home with my IV. I'm a nurse, I can hang my own antibiotics."

Erica threw up her hands in defeat. "Argue with the doctor, okay? Leave me out of it."

When Dr. Feeney walked in a few moments later, he raised a hand as Shelly opened her mouth. "Hold on. Before you start nagging me, I want to ask Dr. O'Connor a few questions."

Shelly snapped her mouth shut, then narrowed her gaze suspiciously. "Why? He doesn't have anything to do with my care."

Jared's jaw tightened, but Shelly chose to ignore it. Okay, so maybe she wouldn't be here without Jared's help, but that didn't give this Dr. Feeney any right to discuss her care with him. It was a privacy violation, wasn't it? But before she could blink, the two men left her alone with her son.

"We had hotcakes and sausage for breakfast," Ty chattered, seemingly not put off with her being a patient in the emergency department. "You should see how much food is in the cafeteria, Mom. There's loads and loads of stuff to pick from. Like, you can ask for anything you want. Anything! Can we stay here for lunch, too?"

Shelly flashed Ty a tired smile. "I don't know, we'll see. I'm glad you enjoyed breakfast. It was nice of Dr. O'Connor to take you."

"Is he your boyfriend?" Ty asked at the exact same moment the two physicians returned to her room.

Mortification burned her cheeks. Good grief, where had Ty gotten such a wild idea? And she didn't even know what thoughts lurked behind Jared's eyes. He raised a brow in her direction, but she was grateful he didn't mention anything about Ty's innocent question.

"Shelly, you'll be glad to know Dr. Feeney is willing to allow you to be discharged, with an IV for your antibiotics. As soon as this dose is in, you'll be released."

"Good." Shelly leaned back against the raised mattress of her gurney. "See, Ty? We'll be home before lunch."

"There's only one condition," Jared added.

Her gut clenched. She should have known Dr. Feeney's capitulation had been too easy. "And what might that be?"

"That you allow me to sleep on your sofa overnight to keep an eye on you." Jared's normally somber gaze twinkled in amusement as her eyes widened in horror. "Don't worry, I promise to behave."

5

B ehave? Maybe she didn't want Jared to behave. She gave herself a mental head-slap. Wait a minute, what was she thinking? Of course, she wanted Jared to behave. The man was too good-looking for his own good. A testosterone-laden complication she didn't need.

The more she thought about it, the more she resented the fact that he planned on staying at her place. She didn't want him hanging around, getting underfoot. Not when she looked terrible with her greasy hair and pale skin. She probably didn't smell very good either.

She forced herself to look him directly in the eye. It was difficult to make a stubborn stand while lying supine on a hospital gurney, but she gave it her best shot. "I'm perfectly capable of taking care of myself. I hang antibiotics for patients every single day. I'm sure I can manage. I'm not an invalid."

"No one said you were." Jared's voice was calm. Reasonable. But she was so not in the mood to be rational.

Giving up on Jared, she turned toward Dr. Feeney. The

older doctor stood with his arms crossed over his chest and a bland, almost bored expression on his face.

"Dr. Feeney, I need to go home. Surely you can understand my dilemma. My son can't stay alone, and I don't have any family to watch over him for me."

"Not even Ty's father?" Jared interjected.

She glared at him, wordlessly telling him to back off. "No." She shifted back toward Dr. Feeney. "I don't understand why this is such a big deal. What could possibly happen to me that would need Dr. O'Connor's attention?"

"Let's see, maybe you've heard of septic shock?" His condescending tone raked like fingernails down a chalkboard against her nerves. "A staph infection is serious. You have two choices." He held up one finger. "Spend the night here in the hospital while your son stays with Dr. O'Connor." He lifted a second finger. "Go home under Dr. O'Connor's care. This infection isn't anything to mess around with. If the antibiotics don't work, you'll get worse. You need to rest, which will be difficult enough with a five-year-old around. Your choice."

Right. Some choice. She momentarily closed her eyes. Could this situation get any worse? Grimacing, she quickly realized she was being totally selfish. Yes, things could absolutely be far worse. Ty could be the one stuck in a hospital bed, seriously ill with irreversible kidney disease. She could be holding a sobbing child while they stuck needles into his arms. She would gladly be sick if it meant Ty would be healthy.

Abruptly she lifted her chin, accepting her fate. "You're right. I choose to go home with Jared. I mean, Dr. O'Connor."

"Good. I'll see about getting your medications ready, especially your IV antibiotics." Dr. Feeney grinned, although the thinning of his lips was more like a smirk as if he enjoyed the role of master puppeteer, manipulating people's lives to his will.

"I'll borrow an IV pole for Shelly to use at home," Jared added cheerfully. "We'll return it when we're finished."

Shelly scowled at both of them. Twenty-four hours. Thanks to Dr. Feeney's infinite wisdom, Jared would be staying in her small house for twenty-four hours.

She was probably overreacting. How bad could it be? Surely, she could put up with anything for that long.

THE MOMENT the three of them entered her home, the magnitude of the situation hit hard. Shelly's spirits sank. Her house only had two bedrooms, and while it was both affordable on her income and perfect for her and Ty, the interior shrank considerably with Jared standing in her living room. The sofa pulled out into a sleeper, but she knew from experience it would take up the entire living space. They wouldn't be able to move without tripping over each other.

Resentment flared. She was so exhausted. The abdominal cramping had returned, forcing her to gauge the distance to the bathroom. The IV fluids had helped dramatically, but every muscle in her body felt as if she'd been tossed in the washing machine with the dial stuck on the highest spin cycle.

She didn't want to deal with Jared. Not when she could barely stand, hanging on to the wall for support.

"Come on, bedtime for you." Normally an order from Jared would have made the hairs on the back of her neck stand straight upright. But now, she didn't have the energy to care, much less to fight.

"Mom's room is over here." Ty was no help, skipping down the short hallway and earnestly opening the door of her bedroom.

She scowled, wanting nothing more than to fall face-first into her bed and stay there for several hours. But what did Jared know about taking care of five-year-old boys? Nothing that wasn't in his *Merck Manual of Pediatric Diseases*, she'd bet.

"I'll rest soon." She forced a smile, hoping it wasn't a grimace. "Right now, I need to call the school to let them know why Ty wasn't in class today."

"I can do that." Jared frowned. "Remember, you need to rest."

"But Ty will need to have lunch soon and . . ." She lost her train of thought. For the life of her, she couldn't think of another reason to stay upright. Although there had to be one, didn't there?

"Shelly." Jared leveled her a stern look. "Ty and I will be fine. Better, in fact, if we don't have to worry about you. I need to get the IV pole from the car set up in your room before your next dose of antibiotic is due. The longer you stand there arguing with me, the longer it will take."

Her vision blurred, her eyes nearly crossing with fatigue. Had she really been up most of the night or had it just seemed like it? Finally, she nodded. "You win. The sofa pulls out into a sleeper. Ty will show you where the school phone number is, and there's food in the fridge." She frowned and tried to remember the last time she'd visited the grocery store. "I think there's food in the fridge. But maybe not."

"Bed. Now." Jared walked toward her, and she instinctively knew he'd carry her if necessary. Her fogged mind played tricks on her because she seemed to know exactly how it would feel to be held by Jared, his strong arms wrapping strongly yet protectively around her.

Her imagination? Or had that really happened? She frowned and moved away, ducking out of Jared's reach, making her way down the short hallway under her own feeble strength. "I'm going. Just take care of Ty." She couldn't completely erase the wistful note in her tone.

Thankfully, Jared didn't follow her all the way to her room. But when she glanced back at him, she noticed he was watching her intently, a puzzled expression on his face. He wasn't a parent, so he couldn't possibly understand how it felt to hand the care of your child over to someone who was almost a stranger.

"I will. I promise, he'll be fine."

Despite her exhaustion and cramping discomfort, Shelly nodded and entered her room. She changed into a clean pair of pajamas, then crawled thankfully into bed. A few minutes later, Jared brought the IV pole in, set it up, and then hung the IV bag on the hook. She wasn't due for the next dose of antibiotic just yet, and he quickly left giving her time alone to rest. But even when she was surrounded by the comforts of her own home, she couldn't lose herself in blessed sleep.

She heard the deep rumble of Jared's masculine voice followed by the delighted peal of Ty's laughter and wondered what Jared had said that was so funny. Ty was no doubt thoroughly enjoying the novelty of masculine attention. For a moment, uncertainty gnawed at her. Had she made the right choice all those years ago? Could she have tried to convince Mark's family to see reason?

Shelly squashed the useless regrets. She knew she'd made the only decision she could have at the time. Single, alone, and pretty much penniless, she couldn't have taken on Mark's wealthy parents and won. Not without a lot of luck.

The risk of losing her child for good had been too steep a price to bet on luck.

Ty was happy. She'd provided a good home for him over the years. She didn't know why God meant for her to raise Ty alone, but she was determined to make the most of the path He had set before her.

Just as she drifted off to sleep, it occurred to her that she'd given Tyler everything he possibly needed.

Except a father.

JARED GRINNED as Ty performed another in a row of somersaults that propelled him across the length of the backyard. The kid possessed a bottomless energy every adult coveted. After displaying his gymnastic expertise, Ty showed off his sturdy swingset by climbing up to the very top.

"See? I told you I could," Ty gloated.

He winced, imagining his feeble explanation to a suspicious ED doctor when Ty ended up in the hospital with a cracked skull. He'd taken care of enough kids to know accidents happened, but they could also be prevented. He gestured for Ty to come down. "I do see, but you need to come down now. Please."

As the afternoon wore on, Jared slowly realized Ty bore an uncanny resemblance to his brother Mark. The boy's brown eyes and brown hair were similar traits to dozens of other kids, but the little things, like the way his eyes crinkled at the corners and the hint of a dimple that flashed in his right cheek when he smiled, took Jared back several years.

He imagined Mark had looked at him the same way Ty did, tilting his head to one side when listening to something Jared was saying.

Absently, Jared rubbed the nagging ache in the center of his chest. He was becoming obsessed with his brother. Memories of Mark had taken up residence in his head, telegraphing intermittent waves of guilt. Even now, he knew he should be searching for Leigh Wilson instead of playing babysitter to Shelly's son.

Jared sighed. Maybe he was kidding himself in thinking he could succeed where the private investigator had failed. He'd already logged several hours on the internet on various search engines to no avail. Today he'd planned to head down to the Milwaukee County Courthouse to search all the Wilsons living here during the time Leigh had been born. He'd hoped to start interviewing them one by one to see if he could find a relative of hers. There had to be an aunt or uncle, if not her parents somewhere.

"Mr. Jared? I'm hungry. What's for supper?"

Good question. Jared looked at his watch, noting with surprise that the time was close to six p.m. It had been a few hours since he'd checked on Shelly. Ty had polished off an afternoon snack then, too, but obviously, the kid needed to eat often to keep up with his speedy bird-like metabolism.

"Let me check with your mom, she's due for her medicine. When I'm finished with that, I'll order pizza." Pizza was safe, wasn't it? Didn't every kid in the world like pizza?

Ty's face clouded, and he shook his head. "I can't have pizza. Mom says it has too much salt in it."

Make that every kid in the world except for Ty. Jared eyed him thoughtfully. He was all for healthy eating, but to ask a kid Ty's age to worry about eating too much salt seemed to push the health notion a bit too far.

Unless there was some sort of physiological reason why Shelly watched the boy's salt intake? Pausing mid-stride, Jared remembered the vague words she'd spoken that day in his office. He'd been upset over his father's heart failure, and she'd been empathetic over how it felt to have someone you loved suffering an illness. When he'd asked more, she'd admitted that she would know more after they ran some tests. He hadn't known about her son at the time, but now he wondered if Ty was the one who needed tests? Was there something wrong with her son?

"I don't really like pizza anyway," he quickly said. "How about a bucket of chicken instead?" There may be salt in the batter, but he felt sure the local deli offered a heart-healthy version.

"Yum." Ty patted his stomach as Jared accompanied him inside the house.

Jared phoned the deli and placed their order, then walked down the hall toward Shelly's room. Although, he reminded himself he was a doctor and she was his patient. At least, for the next twenty-four hours.

Still, he felt like a voyeur as he opened the door to her bedroom and crossed the threshold.

She was sleeping. For a long moment, he stood in the dim room watching her. Despite having been so ill, she was really lovely. Her features were relaxed, yet he clearly remembered the stubborn tilt to her chin when she was awake. Why did she resent needing his help? Or anyone's help for that matter? She wasn't Wonder Woman, although the way she'd fought back while lying on a hospital gurney had been a good imitation of the fearless warrior.

His gaze followed the graceful curve of her jaw, the slender slope of her throat. Realizing what he was doing, he quickly averted his gaze.

Shelly deserved respect. It wasn't her fault he'd bullied his way into her home. As a professional, gawking was strictly forbidden. Especially when the gawkee was asleep in her bed and completely unaware of his presence as the gawker.

Jared didn't want to wake her, but she needed her antibiotic dose. He tiptoed farther into her room and took the mini-bag off the IV pole and connected it to the IV tubing. With the tip in one hand, he frowned, staring down at her as he tried to remember which arm the IV was in.

A nurse would probably remember something like that, he thought with an inward grimace.

Her right arm, he told himself. He was pretty sure the IV was in her right arm.

Afraid of waking her, he gently eased her right arm out from under the blanket. Thankfully, he'd remembered correctly and it didn't take him long to connect the ends of the IV together.

She shifted and mumbled something but didn't wake up. When the IV was dripping appropriately, he gently tucked her arm beneath the blanket, then backed slowly out of her room before silently shutting the door behind him. After this dose, he'd cap her IV so it wouldn't clot off because Shelly wouldn't need another dose until midnight.

Dinner went well, and Jared was feeling pretty good about his role as temporary parent until Ty began to pepper him with questions.

"How come you don't have a little boy of your own?"

"Because I haven't found a woman I love enough to marry and have a family with." He tossed the bones of their chicken in the trash.

"How come you haven't found a woman yet?"

Jared's lips twitched as he fought a grin. Ty was really something. "I don't know, maybe women don't like me."

"Hmm." Ty scrunched up his face in concentration. "You gotta talk nice to women if you want them to like you. No bad words or anything." Ty paused for a few seconds, then added, "Alex's dad brings his mom flowers. Maybe you should try that? I bet a woman would like you if you brought flowers."

"Good idea. I'll remember that one." Jared nodded sagely. "Now why don't you tell me what time you're supposed to go to bed on a school night."

"Eight o'clock, but Mom always lets me stay up later for special occasions."

"Oh, and I bet you think me being here with you is a special occasion, huh?" Jared knew when he was being hosed by a pro.

Ty bobbed his head enthusiastically. "Yep. Can we play a game?"

"Only if you agree to go to bed at your normal time of eight o'clock."

"Aw, do I hafta?"

"Yes. And I'm pretty sure your mom would agree if she were awake." Jared hoped Ty wouldn't put up too much of a fuss. He was feeling pretty exhausted himself. Chasing Ty around had proved to be harder than he'd imagined. He'd have to give parents of small children more credit—heaven knew, they deserved it.

The boy's hopeful expression fell. "I guess."

Jared pulled out the sofa sleeper so they could play the board game on the mattress. Ty jumped up and down on the bed until Jared grabbed him.

"Whoa there, this isn't a trampoline."

"We can make it a trampoline!" Ty yanked himself out of Jared's grasp and proceeded to jump harder and higher.

With a groan, Jared tipped his head back, stared at the ceiling, and wished the hands on the clock would move a little faster. Wasn't it eight o'clock yet? Why had he been stupid enough to mention the word *trampoline*?

He began explaining why they couldn't make the sofa sleeper into a trampoline, but Ty wasn't listening, so he gave up the rational route.

"Stop!" he barked. "No jumping or you'll go to bed right now."

He felt a bit guilty for coming down so hard on him, but Tyler dropped down on the sofa to lean over the game. The kid didn't hold a grudge, and the game went on without any more issues.

Remembering how long Ty had spent in the men's room, Jared decided he should encourage the boy to start getting ready for bed at seven thirty.

Sure enough, Ty couldn't find his favorite pajamas, so they spent ten minutes looking in every dresser drawer because Ty refused to sleep in anything but Spiderman. Ty finally found them deep inside his play-fort that masqueraded as his closet. After the toothbrush ritual and addressing his complaints of being thirsty, the boy finally climbed into his bed.

"Goodnight, Ty."

"Night." Ty's jaw stretched into a wide yawn, then his eyes popped open. "I almost forgot my prayers!"

Jared swallowed a groan. He would have asked Ty to forgo the ritual for tonight but figured neither Shelly nor God would appreciate the brush-off. "You'd better say them, then."

Ty folded his hands under his chin and closed his eyes.

"Dear God, please bless Mrs. Ellen, Alex, Emma, my mom, and my daddy who is up in heaven. Oh, and I almost forgot. Please bless Mr. Jared, too. Amen."

Speechless, Jared stared at Ty. Not only because he was fairly certain he'd never been included in anyone's prayers before, but because of what else Ty had said. His daddy was already up in heaven? Somehow he'd gotten the impression from Shelly that Ty's father was still around somewhere. When had Ty's father died?

He had to ask. Crossing to Ty's bed, he sat down on the edge of the mattress. "Thanks for including me in your prayers, Ty."

"You're welcome." The boy yawned again.

He felt like slime, pumping Ty for information. But it didn't stop him from probing for the truth. "I'm sorry your dad died. I bet you really miss him."

"Yeah." Ty nodded earnestly. "Most the kids at school have daddies, except for Izzy. Her daddy is up in heaven, too."

He didn't know who Izzy was and, at the moment, didn't care. "How long ago did your dad die? A few months ago? Do you remember him?"

"No. My mom says he loved me a lot, but he died before I was borned."

JARED PROPPED his arms behind his head, shifting on the hard mattress of the sofa bed. His thoughts wouldn't stop whirling in his head. Shelly's son was the same age as Mark's child. Both Ty's father and Mark had died before their sons had been born. The similarities between Ty's situation and Mark's long-lost child wouldn't leave him alone.

Shelly's last name was Bennett. Mark's fiancée's name was Leigh Wilson. Shelly was a trained flight nurse, while Leigh had been a cocktail waitress in a nightclub. He couldn't imagine any scenario that made them the same person, but then he'd remember how much Ty reminded him of Mark and the doubts would return.

Of course, the truth would be easy enough to prove one way or the other. He could get a sample of Ty's DNA to be tested in a lab, although that could take months to process. Or he could simply do a background check on Shelly. Was Bennett her maiden name? Or her mother's maiden name? Had she been married at one point? It didn't seem likely, but anything was possible.

For all he knew, there was already a background check in her personnel file at Lifeline. As the medical director, it was his responsibility to know about his employees, right?

Wrong.

He scowled at the ceiling of Shelly's living room. He knew Shelly's personal past wasn't any of his business. Unless she'd committed some sort of crime, which he was certain she hadn't. Unless she was really Leigh Wilson, which was such a remote possibility he couldn't believe he was entertaining the harebrained notion.

He needed his head examined. From the moment he'd met Shelly, he'd been irrationally attracted to her. She'd ripped his concentration to shreds, taking over his every waking thought until he had to force himself to focus on the real reason for being here—to find Leigh and her child. Easy enough to understand why he'd suddenly jumped to the easy answer, combining the two women messing up his head into one.

The creak of a floorboard caught his attention. Holding perfectly still, he strained to listen. Had Ty climbed out of bed? Was he going to his mother? Jared waited, trying to get a clue to the source of the noise.

Was that water running in the bathroom? Had Ty gotten up to go in there or was it Shelly?

He hesitated, unwilling to breach Shelly's privacy. The water stopped, and he thought he heard the door open.

Then nothing.

Everything was quiet. Shelly must have made her way back to bed.

Jared relaxed against the cushions he was using as a pillow. If sleep had eluded him before, it was beyond impossible now.

A slight sound, like the rustle of clothing, had him opening his eyes to peer through the darkness. Then he heard a thud and muffled groan moments before something soft and womanly fell directly on top of him.

6

Shelly grunted as pain zinged up her shin and the breath was knocked from her body. She landed against something firm, wincing when the IV in her right arm tugged uncomfortably beneath its protective dressing.

When strong, steady arms wrapped around her, it took a moment to realize what had happened.

"Shelly? Are you all right?" Jared's deep, rumbling voice in her ear sent shivers down her spine. On one hand, she was grateful she'd fallen on an angle, her outstretched hands missing his body and hitting the mattress as she'd landed. But on the other hand, the position was hardly appropriate with her body on top of his.

"Fine," she whispered, relieved that the darkness hid her flaming red cheeks. Talk about embarrassing! "Sorry, I forgot you were here."

His chuckle, coming from the darkness that surrounded them, warmed her toes. He shifted on the bed and helped her to sit upright so that they weren't sprawled on top of each other. She ran her fingers through her tousled hair and made sure the IV in her hand hadn't pulled loose as she tried to pull herself together.

"Thanks." Was that breathy voice hers? Honestly, she needed to get a grip.

"My pleasure," he said, his arm sliding around her shoulders. "Need help standing upright?"

"Um, no. I'm okay." The warmth radiating from his body seared through her thin, baggy T-shirt she used as sleepwear. Despite her assurances, her knees felt wobbly as she stood. Not from the fall, but from being so close to Jared.

"Lean on me," he encouraged, pulling her close.

Leaning on him was something she shouldn't do, literally or figuratively. But being so close to him felt nice, and she couldn't muster the strength to push him away.

He walked her to the bedroom door, and she'd completely forgotten that she'd been feeling a little hungry and wanted to try a slice of dry toast. Somehow, falling against Jared had wiped away her hunger.

At the doorway to her room, Jared paused and lifted a hand to smooth a strand of hair away from her cheek. "Shelly." Her name was a whispered groan. He kissed her gently, chastely, once, then twice, then a third time, firmer, silently begging for more. She couldn't think, couldn't breathe, there was only Jared. And for the first time in what seemed like forever, the long-forgotten sensation of being held in a man's arms washed over her.

"Sweet," he whispered. "So sweet."

"Mo-om." A thin wail broke through the red haze of desire. "I need you."

Ty? In a heartbeat, she crashed from being halfway to the moon, back to the hard-core reality of earth. She instinctively pushed away from Jared, her thoughts on her son. He didn't try to prevent her from moving toward her son's room.

"What is it, Ty?" As she turned, she belatedly noticed the light shining from the partially open bathroom door right next to his. When she realized what was going on, her heart sank like a stone. She knew exactly why Ty needed her. The symptoms of Ty's ongoing bladder infections were all too familiar.

"I'm here, honey. It's okay."

"It hurts," he whimpered.

Helplessly, she cradled his shoulders as he stood at the side of the toilet. Although the brightness of the light made it hard to see clearly, she thought perhaps his urine was clouding again. "Are you finished?"

"Yeah, but make it not hurt." His plea nearly broke her heart.

"I'll try. I have some medicine here for you. Here, flush the toilet and sit down on the cover. Remember those antibiotics the doctor gave us for this? I have an extra bottle." She rummaged in the medicine cabinet as she spoke, finding the bottle and quickly shaking a pill in her hand. "I need you to chew this up like a big boy."

Ty took the medication, accustomed to the routine by now. He chewed the pill, drank from the glass of water she provided, then handed it back to her.

"Good job," she praised him. "Ready to go back to bed?"

He nodded and slid off the toilet seat.

Shelly guided him across the hall to his room and into bed. She pulled the covers up and tucked them under his chin. Leaning down, she pressed a soft kiss to his cheek. "I love you, Ty. Try to get some sleep."

"I love you, too." He snuggled down into the pillow. "G'night."

"Goodnight. Don't let the bedbugs bite." Shelly blinked the moisture from her eyes, a sinking sensation gnawing at her stomach as she stared down at his innocent face. Another bladder infection was not a good sign. Mentally she counted backward. How many weeks since his last one? Three or four at the most.

The infections were coming more frequently now. Maybe because his body was becoming immune to the antibiotics or because there was something more seriously wrong with him than a simple bladder infection. Only lab testing would tell them for sure if Ty had kidney failure. Shelly tiptoed from his room, closing the door silently behind her. For a moment, she stood, shame washing over her. She hadn't heard Ty get up. Worse, she'd been kissing Jared just a few feet away from Ty's room. What was she thinking?

"Is Ty all right?" Jared's voice came from somewhere behind her. She whirled around, the light from the bathroom door illuminating his concerned features. "Did he have a nightmare?"

"No, but he'll be fine." He must not have heard her giving Ty the antibiotic medication or he would have asked about it.

"Glad to hear it." Jared stepped closer, and his musky scent teased her senses. "And what about you?"

"Me?" Her voice rose in a squeak.

"Yes, you. Are you all right?"

She nodded, even though that wasn't entirely true. "Why wouldn't I be okay?"

His gaze seemed to bore into her. "Having second thoughts about kissing me?"

Yes. No. Maybe.

She drew in a ragged breath. "I, um, don't want you to get the wrong idea, Jared. As a single mother, I have to stay focused on Tyler. I'm not really in the market for a relationship."

"I see." His brow furrowed, and rather than retreating from her, he reached out and took her hand in his. "Can we talk about it?"

The heat of his fingers threatened to melt her resolve. Talking to Jared was just as hazardous as kissing him. He had a way of getting her to reveal too much. His kindness was lethal.

Her starved soul wanted to gobble him up, regardless of the inevitable heartbreak that would follow.

"I need to get some sleep." She wasn't ashamed of taking the coward's way out.

"You must have gotten up originally for some reason," he argued logically.

Her stomach chose that moment to grumble loudly.

"Are you hungry?" His gaze was quizzical.

"Maybe a little." She rubbed her abdomen. Her stomach ached in the way that told her she needed to eat.

"Come on, let's try some toast." Jared gently tugged on her hand, pulling her toward the tiny kitchen table.

"I'm not an invalid," she protested. Dropping his hand, she moved farther into the kitchen and turned the light on over the sink. She pulled out the bread and dropped two slices in the toaster, hyperaware of Jared's presence behind her.

"Do I need to apologize?" His softly spoken question startled her.

"No." She turned to face him. "That kiss shouldn't have happened, but it's hardly your fault."

"Shouldn't have happened?" Jared's voice was mild, but there was no missing the dangerous inflection underlying his tone. "Am I missing something? Are you in a relationship with someone?"

"No!" Her denial was swift, and she forced herself to take a deep breath. "I'm saying this badly. I'm attracted to you, but I don't date. Ever. Tyler is too important to me."

Jared's gaze narrowed. "Now I'm really confused. You dating a man is bad for Tyler because . . . ?"

She lifted her chin, not appreciating the way he was pushing this. "Because I won't have him hurt by a relationship that falls apart. He's too young to understand. He sees his friends' parents happily married and automatically will think that anyone I date is potential father material." When Jared opened his mouth to argue, she held up a hand to stop him. "Besides, this isn't only about Ty. It's about me. I'm not ready for this."

He was silent for a moment. Her bread popped up, and she decided not to tempt fate by adding butter or jam. Nibbling the dry toast, she watched him.

"Because you're still in love with Ty's father?"

It was tempting to agree, but she couldn't lie. Not about this. Not to him. Jared had rushed to her side when she'd called for help. He'd stayed with her, watched over Ty for her. He was a good man, one who deserved the truth.

"No. I'm not pining for Ty's father. Don't ask me to explain something I'm not sure I understand myself." Her gaze implored him to let it go. "Trust me, Jared, it's best if we go our separate ways. Emotionally, I can't do this. I'm sorry."

"Me, too." Jared stood, his lean body within inches of hers. So close she could have leaned against him the way she longed to do. She swallowed hard against a lump of dry toast and averted her gaze. "I'll stay until your last morning dose of antibiotic is in, then I'll get out of your hair."

Perversely, she wanted to beg him not to leave. Instead, she forced a smile. "Thanks for understanding."

He didn't return her smile, his solemn gaze capturing hers. "I don't understand, because your logic is flawed. But I don't push myself where I'm not wanted. Call me if you need anything else."

"I will." Her smile faded because she knew she wouldn't. Couldn't. Or she might end up back in his arms.

"I hope so." His expression was grim as he returned to the living room.

Shelly set her toast aside. Her stomach didn't feel any better, but she knew the nausea wasn't related to the food poisoning. It was because of what she'd just done.

Pushed away the one person who could have been a very good friend.

7

J ared lay on the sofa, eyes gritty from lack of sleep. Watching the sun creep over the horizon through Shelly's living room made him feel helplessly grim, knowing he'd lost something precious. He'd only held Shelly in his arms for a few minutes, but it was enough to imprint the sensation of having her close in his mind, forever.

Enough. He had to stop torturing himself. She wasn't interested, end of story. Bad enough that he'd taken advantage of her weakened condition, what kind of doctor was he anyway? He should have kept his distance.

He shifted on the rock-hard mattress of the sleeper sofa. It had been impossible to wipe those stolen moments with Shelly from his mind. When had he ever felt such an intense need to be with a woman? Not just any woman, but Shelly. Kate's pretty smile didn't hold the least bit of appeal. No, only Shelly had the power to drive him insane. Only Shelly possessed the ability to make him forget all the reasons he was too busy to have a life of his own.

Only Shelly had made him forget about his silent promise to Mark.

He rubbed a weary hand over his eyes. In another hour he could give Shelly her last dose of IV antibiotic. If he were being honest, she was more than capable of giving the medication to herself. Yet, he was determined to see this through. And once he'd given it to her, he'd leave. Today was his scheduled day off, and he had a full day of investigating to do. He should be grateful Shelly had pushed him away. Leigh Wilson was his main priority. Somehow he suspected he would have given up his mission at the slightest encouragement from Shelly.

He hadn't imagined her response, the way she'd kissed him back. She'd fit perfectly against him, not super-slim, all angles and bones, the way some women were. She was soft and full of curves.

Stop. He couldn't keep thinking about this. Shelly was off-limits. She'd told him so herself. She wasn't interested in a relationship, and he shouldn't be either. He needed to quit acting as if he'd lost a best friend. He didn't even know Shelly very well. How could he miss her friendship?

Making an abrupt decision, he swung his legs off the sleeper sofa and levered himself upright. The clock on the wall showed five thirty, which was close enough to six. No reason he couldn't just hang the stupid antibiotic now and be done with it.

Shelly was still sleeping when he tiptoed into her room. He purposefully kept his gaze averted from her relaxed pose, reminding himself he was a professional. The IV pole had been pushed off to the side. He retrieved it and backfilled the mini-bag of medication. When the setup was complete, he held the end of the IV tubing in one hand and sought the arm that held her IV catheter.

Her hands were curled beneath her cheek. The creamy complexion of her skin drew him closer, and his willpower fled as he lightly stroked a finger down the satiny softness. She didn't stir, looking less like the warrior woman he knew her to be. Her features were relaxed, but when she opened her eyes, the green gaze would flash with intense protectiveness toward her son.

Jared mentally slapped himself upside the head. Mooning over something that would never be was a waste of time and energy. With intense determination, he gently eased Shelly's right arm out from the covers, thankful she was lying on her left side. Despite the awkward angle, he deftly unwrapped the dressing over her IV, then connected the tubing together. He opened the clamp and adjusted the rate of the medication.

Mission accomplished. Shelly stirred in her sleep but didn't fully wake up. After double-checking everything was okay, he backed away. With one last glance at her, he retreated from the room, gently shutting the door behind him.

"Mr. Jared?"

He spun around, surprised at Ty's voice coming from behind him. He'd tried to get Ty to call him Jared, but Shelly had instilled respect for adults into the boy, encouraging the use of Mr. or Mrs. Before their first names.

"Ty. What are you doing up so early?"

"I hafta go to the bathroom, but I'm afraid it's going to hurt." His lower lip trembled as he pulled on his pajama shirt, twisting the fabric into a knot.

"Hurt?" Jared had given Shelly and Ty privacy last night, so he hadn't overheard their conversation in the bathroom. But now he realized he'd missed something. "You mean, it hurts when you go?"

Ty's head nodded up and down. "Yeah. My mom gave me medication, but I'm still scared it will hurt."

"I'll come with you." Dazed, Jared gestured for Ty to enter the bathroom ahead of him. "What kind of medicine did your mom give you?"

"It's up there." Ty gestured to the medicine cabinet, the mirrored door hanging slightly ajar. Jared swung it open and spied a small orange pharmacy bottle with Tyler's name on it.

Chewable Bactrim was printed on the label. Medication used for bladder infections. Ty suffered from them? He knew exactly what the boy was going through. He remembered suffering from the same malady as a kid.

Jared waited until the boy had finished going to the bathroom—Ty claimed it still hurt but not as badly—then helped him wash his hands. Despite his vow to leave immediately, Jared ended up making Ty breakfast in the kitchen.

Shelly found them there, an hour later. "Good morning."

"Hi, Mom. Mr. Jared made scrambled eggs and sausage. Do you want some?"

"Er, no, thanks. I'll start with coffee." His heart gave a little pang when she avoided his direct gaze.

"The pot there is fresh, help yourself." He gestured to the carafe.

"Thanks." She helped herself to a mug of coffee. "I disconnected the IV because the antibiotic was infused. I, uh, didn't hear you come in."

Was there an underlying note of reprimand in her tone? A blind man could have seen how badly she wanted him to leave. Out of her house and out of her life.

He set his half-full cup of coffee on the counter. "I didn't want to wake you, but now that you're up, I'll be on my way." He didn't want to go, he wanted to ask about Tyler's bladder infection. How frequently did the boy get them? Was he having tests? If so, when? He opened his mouth, intending to ask more, but then caught himself. "Goodbye, Ty, see you later. Hope you feel better, Shelly."

"Thanks again, Jared." Shelly's voice was soft, but she didn't meet his gaze.

He made his escape with a minimum of fuss.

Shelly and Ty were a tight-knit family unit. One, she'd made clear, that didn't include him.

JARED TOOK the steps to the courthouse two at a time. Although this was his day off, he should have offered to work after spending his entire workday with Shelly the day before, but he refused to give in to the wave of guilt. It was well past time he made some headway in finding Leigh Wilson.

A task proving much easier said than done. He looked through birth records spanning the few years he'd thought Leigh Wilson had been born, guessing she was roughly the same age as Shelly. But his plan of making a list of Wilsons was daunting. There were far too many, even after he tried narrowing his search. He found himself looking for Bennetts instead. Was Bennett Shelly's maiden name? Or a married one?

Groaning inwardly, he told himself to forget about Shelly and Ty. About how their situation was so similar to that of Leigh Wilson. He debated broadening his search to include all the Milwaukee area suburban cities, but that only lengthened his list.

Several hours later, armed with reams of paper listing various Wilsons, he gave up and headed to the deli for lunch. Setting the pile of papers beside him, he propped his elbows on the table and rubbed his temples. What was his next step? He had no clue where to go from here.

He tried to study the list over a sandwich, but the seemingly endless stream of possibilities was overwhelming. With a frustrated move, he shoved them aside. He needed help. This wasn't his area of expertise. He was good at keeping kids alive, not at finding lost or missing women and children. He wasn't skilled enough to do this alone. The last private investigator his dad had hired had failed miserably. But what if he found someone else? Someone here in town where Jared could keep a close eye on his work or lack thereof.

Warming to the idea, he finished his meal and returned home. Using his computer, he searched for private investigators in the Milwaukee area. He spoke to several, doing phone interviews so that the PI would understand his expectations, specifically daily briefings. By the time he got to the last one, the man listened patiently as he explained over the phone about his list of Wilsons in the area and how he'd hoped to locate the whereabouts of Leigh Wilson.

"I understand what you're trying to do, but I think you're going about it all wrong," Brandon Rafter said.

Jared squelched a flash of impatience. None of the other four had told him his methods were off, only assured him that they'd produce results. "Oh really? And just what other option would you suggest?"

"Start with birth records," Brandon advised. "With a full name and birth date, anyone can be found. But without those two pieces of information, you're spitting in the wind."

"I've looked for a birth date and can't find one."

"Are you sure Leigh is this woman's real first name? I've spent hours searching for someone only to find out that the person goes by their middle name, rather than their given first name."

Stunned, Jared stared off into the distance. The idea that Leigh might not be Mark's fiancée's given first name hadn't occurred to him. "I'm not sure," he admitted.

"Look, I've found hundreds of people, performed hundreds of background investigations. I'll give this a shot. I have access to several databases. But I won't make you any promises. Especially since we don't know for sure if this Leigh Wilson was born in Milwaukee under that particular name."

The guy's honesty cemented his decision. "You're hired. I'll pay the initial fee and the balance when you find her."

"Great, thanks. Give me your email and I'll send you an invoice."

Jared rattled it off. "There is something else," he said, ignoring the sharp stab of guilt that pierced the area of his back between his shoulder blades.

"What's that?"

"How much to do another background check?"

Brandon named his price. Jared found himself nodding, even though he knew the guy on the other end of the phone couldn't see him. As much as he didn't have any right to pry into Shelly's personal life, he knew he couldn't focus his attention on Leigh until he'd uncovered the truth about Shelly.

"Okay, that's fair," Jared said. "I'd like you to do a background investigation on Shelly Bennett, flight nurse at Lifeline Air Rescue."

8

S helly gritted her teeth and paced the length of her kitchen while the pediatrician's office put her on hold for the third time. Today was Tuesday. Ty was due back home from school any moment, and she still didn't know if they were supposed to go in for his tests the following morning or not. After what seemed like eons, the nurse came back on the line.

"Ms. Bennett? Dr. Delany asked that your son's testing be delayed until he finishes his course of antibiotics."

"But that won't be until Friday." And she'd already scheduled her work hours around the testing being done tomorrow, not Friday. She was off tonight but was scheduled to work Thursday night on the 1900 to 0730 shift, which meant she'd be dead on her feet to take Ty in for his testing that morning. "Will two days really make any difference? Is there any way I can talk to Dr. Delaney myself?"

"Not until later tonight, this place is crawling with sick kids. I'll ask him to call you when he's finished seeing patients for the day." Her tone wasn't encouraging.

"Thank you." Shelly blew out an exasperated breath and

disconnected from the line. If she waited too long and wasn't able to change the doctor's mind, then she'd be stuck. There was no choice but to go into work to change her schedule. Maybe she could ask Kate or Jess to switch days with her.

Tyler was doing great on the antibiotics, but she really wanted those kidney function tests completed. She needed to understand exactly what future hardships Ty might face. The not knowing day after day was more difficult than hearing definitive news, one way or the other.

"Hi, Mom!" Ty dashed into the house, dropping his book bag carelessly on the floor as he rushed over to give her a hug. "Guess what? I got a star on my story paper."

"You did?" Shelly grinned as Ty bubbled over with excitement. "Let me see."

"It's in my bag. I'm hungry, can I have a snack?"

Ty was a whirlwind of energy. Shelly knew from past experience to let him eat first, before discussing homework. Not that the kindergarten teacher often gave much in the way of homework, other than the standard nightly reading session that she and Ty enjoyed so much that it hardly counted as work.

She busied herself with setting out Ty's snack, then glanced at the clock. There was time after Ty's snack to run over to Lifeline before dinner.

"Can we have Mr. Jared over for dinner?" Ty's eyes pleaded with her as he dipped his slice of apple into the caramel and took a bite. "Please?"

Shelly was running out of excuses to give him. Ty had apparently grown close to Jared in the short time he'd watched over her son. Five days had passed since her bout of food poisoning, and she'd only seen Jared in passing. Yet, he'd taken up residence in the back of her mind. During the darkest hours of the night, she replayed their kiss over and over again. Sometimes she imagined what would have happened if she'd told Jared she was open to a relationship.

Each time Ty brought up the subject of Jared, though, she knew she'd made the right decision in letting him go. Look how attached her son had grown after a few measly hours. She couldn't bear to imagine what might happen if she allowed herself to get tangled up with Jared and things ended badly between them.

Tyler would be devastated. Mark had died before Ty had been born, so her son hadn't felt the acute loss of his father. She had no idea how Ty would react to losing a father figure now that he was old enough to understand and feel the impact of such an event.

"Not tonight, sweetie. I think Mr. Jared has to work. Finish your snack, because I need to run a quick errand."

"Okay." Ty gobbled up the apple slices and caramel snack in record time.

In an effort to keep busy, she took Tyler with her to Lifeline to check the schedule. Sure enough, Kate was scheduled to fly the night shift of Wednesday night but was off Thursday. If Kate would switch shifts with her, she'd be golden.

Ty went over to talk to Reese who cheerfully responded to her son's eager questions about flying while she called Kate.

"Hi, Kate, I need a huge favor. Any chance you'd swap Wednesday night for Thursday? I need to get Ty to the doctor Friday morning."

"Sure," Kate readily agreed. "No problem. I don't have any big plans this week anyway."

"Great." Shelly blew out a sigh of relief. "I owe you one."

"Nah, just take care of that cute son of yours." Kate

disconnected from the line before Shelly could say anything more.

Relieved to have that done, she made the changes on the master schedule, then went out to find Ty. Her steps slowed when she found him with Jared who was dressed in street clothes, instead of his usual flight suit. She winced, realizing she'd inadvertently told Ty a lie.

Jared wasn't working today after all.

"Hi, Shelly." Was it her imagination or did his gaze hold a hint of longing? "How are you feeling?"

"Much better, thanks." Because of her illness, her work-days had gotten off track, so she hadn't flown as much with Jared as she originally had been scheduled. And now she'd changed her upcoming shift, too. Fate was obviously giving her a helping hand in avoiding Jared as if reinforcing that her decision to stay away from him was the right thing to do.

"Mom, Mr. Jared said he'd love to have dinner with us." Ty dipped and swirled a small toy helicopter, one Reese must have given to him.

Her eyes widened with dismay. "Ty, I don't have anything planned for dinner. I thought we'd stop on the way home to pick up something." She could feel her cheeks burning with embarrassment. Not easy being caught red-handed in a fib.

"There's a restaurant down the road a bit that caters to families." Jared's smile didn't quite reach his eyes, and she hid a wince. The white lie hung heavy between them. "My treat."

"Jared?" Jessica poked her head out of the debriefing room. "Dr. Evans called to see if you would mind working his night shift tonight and tomorrow night. His wife just went into labor."

Saved by the birthing mother, Shelly thought with relief as Jared nodded. "Of course. He warned me her time was near. Tell him not to worry about the night shifts and to let us know how things go. I'm rooting for a girl at eight pounds to win the baby pool."

"Will do, but I have a boy coming in at seven pounds eight ounces, so I'm going to win the pool." Jess laughed before ducking back out of the room.

"Sorry, Ty. I guess we'll have to do this another time." Jared smiled at her son, placing his hand on Ty's shoulder. "Take care and listen to your mom, okay?"

"I will." Ty was disappointed, but he didn't put up a fuss as they left the hangar. To make up for it, and to ease her guilty conscience, Shelly took him to the family restaurant Jared had suggested. Ty appreciated the kid-friendly atmosphere, but she knew he would have enjoyed himself more if Jared had come along with them.

That night, Ty included Jared in his nightly prayers, and Shelly felt the fissure in her heart widen. Her son missed having a father figure in his life, and she was at a loss as to what to do about it.

When she was alone in her room, she took out her journal. She hadn't written an entry in almost a week, but she needed to pen one now.

Mark, there are thousands of single mothers in the world raising children on their own, but how do they manage to make up for the absence of a father? I can't bear the thought of Ty being hurt, but at the same time, he clearly yearns for a male role model to look up to.

Then there's the issue of his potential illness. Even if I found someone to love, someone I could imagine spending the rest of my life with, is that really fair when the road of Ty's future will be filled with rocks and boulders? Even the strongest of marriages have caved under that level of pressure.

I want to give Ty the best chance at a normal life, but at what emotional cost? Is it better for Ty to live without a father or to have a father that he loves then loses? Neither option is acceptable, yet it's a decision I could be forced to make.

I would gladly forsake my own happiness if it meant giving Ty what he needed. Times like this, I really wish I had someone else to talk to.

Shelly.

∾

THE NEXT NIGHT, she left Ty with his friend, Alex, and headed into work. When she saw Jared seated in the debriefing room, her pulse kicked up a notch, belatedly remembering he was here, covering for Rick Evans.

"So what's the news on Mrs. Rick Evans?" She helped herself to a cup of coffee. Working the graveyard shift shot her sleep cycle off-kilter, and she'd need the caffeine to get through the next twelve hours. She'd tried to take a nap while Ty was at school but hadn't slept well.

"Baby girl, Clarise Marie Evans, seven pounds, two ounces." Jared gestured toward the white grease board where the baby pool was written. "Guess what? You won fifty dollars. You beat me out by guessing closest to the weight."

"I did? Wow. I'll put that in my hot water heater fund. Maybe I should buy a lottery ticket," she joked.

Jared frowned and was about to stay something when their pilot, Dirk, came into the room to begin the debriefing.

She didn't have time to wonder what Jared had been about to say because shortly after the debriefing, their first call came in.

"Seven-year-old needing an ICU-to-ICU transfer to Children's Memorial. He's highest on the list for a liver transplant, and they have a match." Shelly read the page out loud.

"Let's go," Jared said.

Dirk had just finished telling them the weather conditions, which were good for flying, so they simply grabbed their gear and made their way to the chopper. Once airborne, Shelly listened as Dirk went over the flight plan.

Their destination hospital wasn't far, only a thirty-minute flight. Shelly remembered once flying seven hours to Michigan to pick up a pediatric patient who needed to come to Children's Memorial for a heart transplant.

Even with their gear and helmets on, she was keenly aware of Jared sitting beside her. She couldn't imagine sitting beside him like this during a fourteen-hour round trip. Small doses of him were difficult enough. Fourteen hours and her nerves would be shot.

Shelly kept her attention focused on the view out the window, although the chances of geese flying at night were non- existent. Still, her job was to help the pilot keep an eye out for any flight hazards, and if that meant staring out the window instead of talking to Jared, then that's exactly what she'd do.

As if he sensed her reluctance to chat, Jared remained silent as well. Or maybe he was angry with her. He'd greeted her cheerfully enough, but now things were strained between them. She didn't understand since he'd seemed willing, almost anxious to take them out for dinner when Ty had asked.

"ETA five minutes," Dirk announced through the headset.

"Roger that." Shelly pulled the flight bag toward her and double-checked the equipment. The shift prior to theirs should have restocked the bag, but she wanted to make sure.

If something crucial was missing, they could restock at the hospital if needed.

"Prepare to land." Dirk was older than Reese with many more flight hours logged under his belt. But in her opinion, his landing was bumpy compared to what she experienced when Reese was in the pilot's seat.

She and Jared disembarked from the chopper and wheeled the gurney inside. Their patient, Craig Adams, lay listlessly in his bed. His skin was an eerie shade of orange— Shelly was shocked at how jaundiced he was. The poor kid clearly needed a new liver to survive.

His mother sat beside him, her expression sad but hopeful. Shelly flashed her a reassuring smile as she approached the bedside. "Hi, Craig. We're here to take you to Children's Memorial." She covered his thin arm with her hand. "Have you ever flown in a helicopter before?"

Craig turned his head toward her, and she wanted to weep when she realized just how sick he was. His breathing was shallow, his pulse far too high. Even the whites of his eyes were yellow. "No." His voice was pathetically weak.

"Well, you're in for a treat." She had to push the words past her constricted throat. The poor child looked so awful she could only imagine how much worse he must have felt. While she talked, she quickly switched the lines and cables over to their portable monitoring equipment while Jared spoke to the transferring physician. "You'll be able to tell all your friends how you flew in the Lifeline helicopter."

"Won't they be jealous?" his mom gamely added.

The corner of Craig's mouth tipped up in a smile. Shelly wondered how long he'd been waiting for a liver transplant. Obviously, too long. She swallowed hard. Would this be Tyler in a few years? Too sick to move as he waited for his kidney transplant?

Don't do this, she warned herself sharply. Tyler doesn't have liver failure. Kidney dialysis wasn't the greatest option in the world, but it was a decent bridge to a transplant. There wasn't an artificial bridge to a new liver. This boy needed a liver transplant or he would die.

Did Craig's mother know how serious the situation was? By the hopeful expression in her eyes, Shelly wasn't certain. Surgery in and of itself was always a risk. Anesthesia, bleeding, infection—the complications were many. And once he made it through surgery, he'd have to take a boatload of medication to keep his tiny body from rejecting the new organ. All transplant patients—heart, lung, liver, or kidney—had to take the same antirejection medication.

Her fingers fumbled with the IV tubing. She blinked, trying to focus. Jared reached around her and gently took the tubing from her hands.

"I've got it." His voice was kind and gentle as if he sensed her inner turmoil.

Her smile of gratitude was brittle. She longed to lean on him, to verbalize her worst fears, but this wasn't the time or the place. Craig needed her. This transplant was needed in order for him to survive to see his eighth birthday.

"Ready?" Jared asked.

"Yes."

"Let's go."

Jared told Craig's mother they would meet her at Children's Memorial hospital, reinforcing the rule against parents riding along. Once they were back up on the helipad and had Craig loaded safely in the helicopter, years of training took over. She and Jared fell into a well-executed rhythm.

Shelly placed the patient headphones over Craig's ears,

then pushed the button on her microphone. "Craig? Can you hear me?"

The boy's yellow eyes widened with excitement, and he nodded. She smiled. "Good. If you need anything, just let us know. We can hear you, too. First, we need to listen for a minute while the pilot takes off."

"Ready for takeoff," Dirk intoned over the intercom.

"We're ready back here," Jared responded.

Craig seemed to enjoy the novelty of flying, and after they reached their cruising altitude, Shelly helped prop up his shoulders so he could look out the window.

"The lights are so pretty," he whispered.

Shelly gently squeezed his bony shoulders, her heart breaking over how thin and weak he was. "Yes, they are," she agreed.

The only problem they encountered during the flight was a mild bout of motion sickness. Jared gave Craig medication to ease his nausea, and he felt better by the time they were approaching Children's Memorial.

"We're almost there," Shelly encouraged the boy as Dirk announced their ETA of five minutes.

"That was fun," Craig said with a weak smile.

"I'm glad." Shelly blinked away the tears that threatened, hoping and praying that Craig would survive long enough to brag to his friends about how he'd ridden in the Lifeline helicopter.

JARED WATCHED Shelly as closely as he watched over their young patient. Something was wrong, she seemed distracted, emotional. Just as he was wondering if he needed to ground her from flying, she quickly grabbed his arm.

"Craig's breathing is worse," she said. "I noticed a five-second pause between breaths. His pulse oximeter readings are okay, but I think he's retaining carbon dioxide. I think he needs to be intubated and don't want to wait until we get to the PICU."

As she spoke, she pulled the necessary equipment out of their flight bag.

Jared nodded, taking the laryngoscope and the endotracheal tube from her fingers. They were already starting to land, but he'd rather intubate now, in the chopper, than in the middle of the hospital elevator.

"Dirk, make it a smooth approach. We're intubating back here. Shelly, give him a milligram of versed and then use the Ambu bag to give several deep breaths."

Shelly gave the medication, then provided two deep breaths. Jared use the scope to visualize Craig's vocal cords, then proceeded to place the breathing tube. Shelly placed a device on the end of the tube to verify placement, then taped it into place.

"We're down," Dirk informed them.

"Just in time," Jared murmured. He and Shelly quickly pulled Craig out of the helicopter, then got him into the pediatric ICU. Upon arrival, Jared insisted they draw an arterial blood gas. He was relieved to know that the boy's levels were abnormally low but weren't as bad as he'd initially thought. Placing the breathing tube had been the right thing to do.

"Ready?" he asked, looking at Shelly.

She nodded, although she seemed loath to leave. Their pagers went off, indicating they had another call. They rushed back out to the chopper and were in the air within ten minutes. But almost as soon as they reached flying height, the call was canceled. Dirk banked the helicopter and headed back to the hangar.

"Lifeline to base, what was the reason for the cancelation?" Jared asked. The call had been for a severely premature infant to be transported to the neonatal intensive care unit.

"Baby took a turn for the worse," the base dispatcher informed him. "Survival is doubtful, so the emergency transport was canceled."

He felt bad about the baby, but some things just weren't meant to be. "Roger that, ten-four."

Shelly continued to appear withdrawn when they returned to the hangar. Jared let her stew for a while before he couldn't stand it a moment longer.

"Shelly, what's wrong?" He didn't tap-dance around the issue; the next call could come in at any moment. "You're not in any condition to fly."

"What?" A green spark flared in Shelly's eyes, and she straightened her shoulders. He wanted to applaud with approval at her instant reaction. "Of course, I can fly. Why would you question my ability to care for patients?"

"You've been seriously preoccupied since we responded to Craig's call. I wasn't sure who I needed to worry about more, you or Craig." Jared gestured toward the sofa. "Talk to me. Are you worried about Ty?"

"I—yes." Shelly momentarily rubbed her eyes. "I'm fine to fly, honest. I'd never risk any harm coming to my small patients."

He held her gaze, waiting for more.

She squirmed, then sighed. "I'm a little worried about Ty, that's all. He has some testing scheduled on Friday morning."

Pleased with her admission, he gentled his tone. "What sort of tests? I know he had a bladder infection several days ago, but that's not totally uncommon in kids. I had a series of bladder infections when I was young, but eventually grew out of them."

"You did?" Her eyes widened with interest. "What happened? How did you grow out of them?"

"Well." He cleared his throat and told himself there was nothing to be embarrassed about. "My right ureter was crooked when I was born. It eventually straightened out, and the infections went away." He reached over to take Shelly's hand. "I'll go with you to Ty's tests if you like."

She didn't answer right away but stared at their joined hands. He ached to pull her into his arms. When she finally spoke, her voice was so low he had to strain to listen.

"I suspect Ty's problems are more serious than that. During his last routine checkup, the pediatrician told me his kidney lab values were on the high side, heading toward abnormal. Based on his history with the bladder infections, the doctor recommended additional testing. Seeing Craig so sick, waiting for a transplant, was like visualizing Ty's worst-case scenario."

"Shelly, as a nurse I can understand why you're thinking the worst. But you also know that the chances are good that Ty will be fine." His thumb stroked the back of her hand. Her skin was soft, and he remembered their embrace as if it were yesterday. She'd haunted him in the days they'd been apart. He'd missed her, more than he thought possible.

Had she missed him? He suspected not. The Wonder Woman persona had returned. She was one of the strongest women he'd ever known.

"Maybe. But with his creatinine on the high side, it's hard not to suspect the worst. Lately, being surrounded by these sick kids has started to bother me." She hesitated, shrugged. "It may be time for a career change."

"Don't jump to leaving pediatric nursing just yet." Jared tried not to show his panic. Shelly was a great peds nurse, one he'd hate to lose. "Sick kids are always more difficult to care for, that's why they're so rewarding."

"Yes. But you mentioned I looked preoccupied and that's concerning."

"You also picked up on Craig's abrupt respiratory decline," he was quick to point out. "You're an excellent nurse, Shelly. Don't be so hard on yourself. I'm sure you'll feel better once Ty's testing has been completed. I'd really like to be there for you on Friday."

"Thanks, but I'll be fine." She gave his hand a slight squeeze, then gently pulled away. He tried not to grind his teeth in frustration. Why was she so determined to do everything alone? Why couldn't she accept his support, even as a friend?

Or as more than a friend?

"I care about Ty, too." He tried one last time to make her understand. She held herself aloof, but he craved so much more. "He's a great kid. Will you at least call me when his test results come back?"

"I—yes. Of course. I'll let you know his results." She sent him a perplexed look. "I didn't realize you two were so close. Ty talks about you all the time."

"He does?" Jared couldn't prevent a broad smile from creasing his face. "He's a good kid, but of course, you already know that. I liked spending time with him. Having a masculine influence in his life can't hurt, right?"

"Really?" Green flames sparked from her eyes, and she jumped up from her seat beside him, planting her hands on her hips. It was a sign of his total and complete madness that he wanted to pull her close and kiss her senseless. "And I suppose you're offering to take on that role? Thanks, but no thanks. I think I know what's best for my son. For your information, I recently enrolled him in a big brother, big sister program. He'll have a male role model. One that I don't need to be personally involved with."

"I wasn't expecting that . . ." But he was talking to the wind. Shelly had already spun around and walked away. Jared stared after her for a moment, letting her go. He hadn't meant to offer to be Ty's father figure, but the more he'd thought about it, the more he warmed to the idea. Of course, he should have known Wonder Woman had already taken matters into her own hands.

At the end of their shift, Jared stayed in his office for a while to get caught up on some paperwork. The private investigator he'd hired to do the background check was due to report in at nine. Elbows propped on his desk, Jared held his head in his hands, fighting exhaustion.

When the phone rang, he jerked awake. Groggy and half-asleep, he picked up the phone. "Dr. O'Connor."

"This is Brandon Rafter. I have some interesting news about Shelly Bennett's background check."

"You do?" Guilt warred with keen interest, and his exhaustion vanished. He hesitated, knowing he was about to cross a line. Shelly would never forgive him if she ever found out he'd pried into her personal life. Just as he was about to tell Brandon to keep the information to himself, the PI continued.

"Shelly Bennett didn't exist until six years ago when she moved to Milwaukee and formally changed her name. Her original name was Sharon Leigh Wilson." The PI let out a bark of laughter. "Can you believe it? Shelly Bennett is the woman you hired me to find."

9

Stunned speechless, Jared blinked. It took several moments for the words to penetrate his brain.

"Are you absolutely certain?" He must have heard it wrong. Or misunderstood.

"I'm sure. Shelly's birth name is Sharon Leigh Wilson," Brandon repeated. "Trust me, I couldn't make something like this up."

Shelly was Leigh? Ty was his nephew? "I don't understand. Shelly is a nurse. How could she have a different name?"

"Sharon legally changed her name six years ago to Shelly Bennett. Bennett is her mother's maiden name. I have to be honest, I'm not sure I would have found her so easily if you hadn't asked for a background check on Shelly Bennett. That's when the red flags started going off."

"Does it say how long she's been a nurse?" he asked, still grappling with the news. Ty was Mark's son. His nephew.

Shelly had once loved his younger brother.

"Looks like four and a half years. It appears she legally changed her name while in her last year of nursing. It's not illegal to change your name, and she went through the proper channels. If you had told me that Leigh Wilson was in a nursing program, we could have found her sooner through the state licensing board."

He hadn't known Leigh was working her way through school. Mark had never mentioned that. All they'd known was that she worked as a cocktail waitress in Boston. Maybe if his father had hired a decent private investigator, they would have known about Shelly a long time ago.

His father. Jared ran his fingers over his hair. He needed to call his parents, let them know he found Leigh, AKA Shelly.

"Thanks, Brandon," he finally said, breaking the silence. "I'll send the balance of your fee today. You've more than earned it."

"Let me know if you need anything else," Brandon Rafter said.

"I will." Jared disconnected from the line, then stared at the phone for a long moment before dialing his parents. It wasn't too early, considering their eastern time zone, but he didn't think they'd mind.

His mother answered on the first ring.

"Mom, are you sitting down?"

"Why, do you have bad news for me?" Her voice sounded uncertain.

"Good news for you. But I still think you'd better sit down."

"Oh dear." Her voice grew faint, and he imagined her sinking bonelessly into a kitchen chair. "Are you telling me what I think you're telling me?"

Jared had to smile. "Yes. I found her. Leigh Wilson has changed her name to Shelly Bennett, and she has a five-year-old son, Tyler. I found Mark's son."

His mother burst into tears. Jared expected the reaction, but hearing her heartfelt sobs a thousand miles away while unable to comfort her shook him anyway.

"Really? Have you seen him? Does he look like Mark?"

"Yes, I've seen him, and he's a miniature version of Mark." Jared remembered the similar facial expressions on Ty's face and how they'd reminded him of his brother. Why hadn't he known on some instinctive level that Ty shared his blood? On the heels of that thought came the jarring truth.

His vision had been clouded by Tyler's beautiful mother. The signs were so obvious now that he looked back, but how was he to know Leigh Wilson had become a flight nurse?

"When can we see him?" his mother demanded. "How soon can you bring him to Boston?"

Whoa, things were moving quicker than he'd anticipated. Although, he should have figured this would be his parents next request. "Soon, Mom, I promise. I've seen Tyler for myself, but he doesn't know about you and Dad yet. In fact, Shelly doesn't know I figured out she's really Leigh Wilson."

"I don't care what it takes, Jared, we want to see our grandson. As soon as humanly possible. That woman has kept him from us long enough."

Jared was taken aback by the hard edge to his mother's tone but understood that she was worried because of his dad's poor health. "Give me time to work things out," he said. "I promise you and Dad will be able to see Tyler very soon. I need a few days to talk to Shelly, but I'm sure she'll be reasonable. Now take care and I'll be in touch."

"Okay, Jared. But your father needs this. Don't make us wait too long."

"I won't." He disconnected from the phone, then sat back

in his chair. His previous exhaustion returned with a vengeance, and he struggled to think clearly. Shelly was a reasonable person; she didn't seem like the type to isolate Ty from his family. Yet that was exactly what she'd done. Six years ago, pregnant with his brother's child, she'd run from Boston to hide out in Milwaukee. She'd gone a step further, legally changing her name making it nearly impossible to find her. Why had such drastic steps been necessary? Had Shelly been so freaked out by the unplanned pregnancy that she'd panicked? Had she been ashamed about being pregnant outside of marriage?

That had to be it; nothing else made sense.

He dug the heels of his hands into his eyes, trying to corral his wild thoughts. There was only one way to know for sure what had gone through her mind all those years ago and that was to ask Shelly herself. But that wasn't an option at the moment. She was home sleeping, the same way he should be.

Jared went online to pay the rest of Brandon's fee, then pushed back from his desk. Rather than risk getting behind the wheel, he went into the small on-call room, barely larger than a cardboard box, containing a narrow bed and bedside table.

He only needed a few hours of sleep, then he'd go see Shelly. His timing was awful, springing this on her when Ty was scheduled for testing the following morning, but this couldn't wait. His parents had dreamed about seeing their lost grandchild for six years, and his father's heart condition was tenuous at best.

His mother was right. They'd waited long enough.

JARED SLEPT for four hours before the ringing phone woke him up. He grabbed it a nanosecond too late. Whoever was on the other end of the line had hung up. It was an unknown number, so he didn't try calling back. Muttering under his breath, he considered putting the phone on silent but then changed his mind. Shelly may need him, and he wouldn't want to miss her call.

He flopped back down on the bed, trying to fall back asleep. But the night of Mark's death played over and over in his mind. What if he'd handled that night differently? He knew deep in his gut that if they hadn't argued, Mark wouldn't have stormed off in anger. And maybe his brother wouldn't have died. Jared hadn't found out until reading the autopsy report that Mark had been drinking. He should have figured it out from his brother's lack of logic, but he had been blinded by his own anger. Mark had interrupted him while he'd been studying for his pediatric boards, the ones he was scheduled to take the following morning. He'd been annoyed at Mark for interrupting him, ranting once again about how narrow-minded their parents were.

Jared had brushed him off, told him to grow up and get a life. Mark had stormed off, driving away in anger, and had ultimately slammed his car against a concrete highway divider, killing him on impact.

The last words he'd said to his brother wouldn't leave him alone.

Closing his eyes on a groan, Jared tried not to dwell on the past, but it was a useless effort. In his dreams, he replayed the events with a different ending. One where Mark didn't leave but calmed down enough to stay overnight, sleeping on the sofa.

But wishing didn't change the past. There was so much he needed to atone for. He hadn't just lost a brother that night, his parents had lost a son, Shelly had lost her fiancé, and Tyler had lost his father.

So much loss from one argument.

Shelly and Mark. Mark and Shelly. She must have loved his brother very much to have vowed to raise Tyler on her own . . .

The phone rang again, jarring him from his doze. This time he managed to answer it in time.

"Yeah?" He didn't care if he sounded rude. If he heard a telemarketer's voice on the other end of the connection, rude wouldn't begin to cover his response.

"Dr. O'Connor? This is Dr. Jacoby, your father's cardiologist. I need your help."

Jared frowned and sat upon the edge of the bed. He'd spoken to the cardiologist several times over the past few weeks about his father's condition. With his father's permission, of course.

"My help? With what?"

"Your father is making arrangements to fly to Milwaukee against my advice. At the very least, I'd like him to undergo another echocardiogram before traveling so far. But he's refusing treatment at this time."

Refusing treatment? Flying to Milwaukee? Jared dropped his head into the palm of his hand, unable to believe how things were spiraling out of control. "I'll talk to him."

"You'd better hurry," Jacoby advised. "From what I could tell, he and his wife are trying to book the first available flight out of Boston."

SHELLY TOSSED and turned the entire night before Ty's tests.

Partially, she was sure, because her sleep cycle was all messed up. But deep down, worry gnawed at her over what the tests might reveal. In a few hours, she'd know if Ty was okay or if he needed more testing because his kidney function remained abnormal.

Twice she'd picked up her journal, only to set it aside without writing a word. The words simply wouldn't come, and she realized she was tired of her one-sided conversations with Mark. As much as she'd once loved the freedom of spilling her thoughts on paper, it wasn't enough. Instead, she battled the ridiculous urge to call Jared. He, more than anyone, would understand her concern. Her inability to sleep.

He'd offered to come with her to the testing, and she couldn't for the life of her figure out why she'd turned him down.

Staring blankly up at the ceiling, her thoughts continued spinning through her mind. Jared was a great guy. She respected his expertise as a physician, yet he didn't carry the sense of arrogance or entitlement that so many of his colleagues did. He listened to her and had the uncanny ability to gauge her moods. He'd dropped everything to help her out when she'd been sick.

And the man definitely knew how to kiss.

The minute she was close to him, every sense went on red-alert. She couldn't remember ever being so in tune to another person. Intimacy had been easy to avoid since losing Mark. She hadn't been interested in other men. Being close to them. Sharing her life with them.

Until Jared.

And wasn't that the biggest problem of all? Her feelings for Jared went deeper than simple attraction. She didn't know if it was his internal strength, his innate sense of honesty, his ability to read her so clearly, or a combination of all three that had sucked her in.

She was definitely hooked.

Telling him about Ty's illness had been liberating. He'd held her hand, caressed the back of it with his thumb. And she'd felt so connected to him on a deeper, subliminal level that scared her into pulling away.

Now she regretted her actions. At the time, everything had been so confusing, her emotions a tangled wreck.

Yet, she longed to see him. To talk to him. To share her fears over Ty's tests with him. To hear his deep reassuring voice.

Was it too early to call? To ask him to come along to the testing?

Her alarm jangled, and she flew upright, slamming her palm on top of the clock to silence it. Maybe after she showered and dressed, just before she left for the hospital she'd call him. Maybe just hearing his voice would be enough to calm her nerves.

An hour later, after feeding Tyler his breakfast and getting them both ready to go, she gathered her courage and called his cell. But the call went through to his voice mail. She left a message, and then set her phone aside.

But by the time she and Ty were on their way to the hospital, Jared hadn't returned her call.

WAITING WAS A KILLER. How did families put up with this every single day? She worked in the medical field and still couldn't tolerate watching the seconds tick by into yet still longer minutes.

Finally, Tyler was finished with his tests. Dread warred

with anticipation as she waited for the doctor to come and see her.

"Ms. Bennett? I'm Dr. Orlando, the nephrologist who ordered and reviewed your son's tests. So far, Tyler's preliminary results look good, but the radiologist still needs to do the final reading on the renal ultrasound. I'm afraid he won't get to that until later today."

"Like how much later?" She couldn't hide her dismay. To have waited all week only to be forced to wait longer seemed unreasonably cruel.

"Well." He shrugged. "For sure by the end of the day."

She glanced up at the clock. It was already past eleven in the morning, and she was sure the end of the day meant as late as five in the evening. "But that's almost six hours from now."

"It may not take that long," he assured her. "That's the worst-case scenario."

She stared at him. Did he really expect her to wait another six interminable, potentially life-altering hours?

"Can't you put a rush on this? Please?" She clutched his arm in a desperate grip. "We've been waiting so long. I really need to know the results."

"I'll see what we can do." He patted her hand as if she were a small child, then stepped away.

Shelly curled her fingers into fists as she watched him go. Six more hours? How on earth would she stand it?

Rather than head home, Shelly stopped at Ty's favorite fast-food joint to pick up lunch, then headed to the park for an impromptu picnic. Ty seemed oblivious to her lack of enthusiasm, enjoying himself on the playground equipment. When she'd looked at her watch for the tenth time in as many minutes, she ripped it off her wrist and stuffed it in the pocket of her jeans.

Don't think the worst, she told herself sternly. The preliminary tests looked good. Why not take that as a really good sign? She tipped her face to the sun, enjoying the warmth against her skin.

If the tests were normal, they could celebrate tonight. She'd call Jared and invite him over. Maybe pick up Ty's favorite ice cream for dessert.

She pushed Ty on the swings, grinning as he squealed in delight. Then she purposefully took her time heading home, stopping at the grocery store to pick up a few things. That was when she noticed her cell phone had a missed call on the screen. It had been set on silent while she was in the hospital, and she'd forgotten to put it back on sound alert.

What if Dr. Orlando had called? She quickly scanned the missed calls, but there were none from the hospital.

Jared had left a message, though, so she listened to that.

"Shelly? It's Jared. I'd really like to talk to you. Please call me when you get in."

She blushed at the wave of pleasure that washed over her. He'd called her back! He hadn't mentioned her message, but he'd called her back.

Deciding against calling him from the grocery store, she decided to wait until she got home. And even then, she thought it might be smart to wait until they'd gotten the final test results.

She made tacos for dinner, keeping an eye on the clock. At quarter to six, just as they were finishing their meal, her cell rang. She pounced on it. "Hello?"

"Ms. Bennett? Tyler's kidney function test results are perfectly normal."

"Normal?" Her heart swelled with relief. "You're sure?"

"Of course." He sounded surprised she'd asked.

"Thank you!" With a war-whoop, she dropped her

phone on the counter and let loose with a wild dance around the kitchen.

Ty was fine! Healthy and fine! Whoo-hoo, Ty was going to be just fine!

"Mom?" Her son slanted her a perplexed look. "Are you going crazy?"

She dropped her head back and let out a true, heartfelt laugh of relief. "Yep. I'm crazy, Ty. Giddy with happiness."

He scrunched up his face. "What's giddy?"

"Me. I'm giddy. We're going to celebrate. Let's get out our party hats." She grabbed his hand and tugged him down the hall to her room.

"Is it my birthday?" Ty looked confused when she pulled out the old box of New Year's party hats and noisemakers. She plopped a hat on his head and blew a party horn in his direction. "Am I six years old now?"

"Nope, it's not your birthday or mine either." She knew Ty was clueless as to the seriousness of the testing he'd undergone, but she wasn't. And they absolutely deserved to celebrate. "We're going to have a party!"

"Can we invite Mr. Jared?"

"You bet. Let's go." She handed him a noisemaker and led the way back to the kitchen. But when she called Jared, he once again didn't pick up. This time, she decided against leaving another message. No point in playing phone tag. He'd see her missed call and hopefully call her back.

Determined to have fun, Shelly pulled up her music app on her phone, then grabbed Ty's hand. "Come on, buster, let's dance."

Ty didn't need any encouragement. He eagerly joined in with her enthusiastic swaying to some oldies but goodies music.

"Celebrate, celebrate, dance to the music . . ."

"Mom!" Ty blew his horn to get her attention. "Someone's at the door."

"Really?" She turned the volume down on her phone and danced her way to the door. Her pulse spiked when she saw Jared standing there.

"Hi!" She flashed him a broad smile, opening the door wide to let him in. "You're just in time for ice cream!"

"Hi yourself." Jared raised his eyebrows when she stuck the noisemaker in his face and blew it at his nose. "Are we celebrating your birthday?"

"No, silly. We're celebrating the fact that Ty's tests came back normal!" She spun in a little circle, shuffling her feet. "Grab yourself a hat and join the fun."

"Shelly." He grabbed her arm, preventing her from dancing away. Her heart soared when he clasped her to him in a quick hug. "I'm so happy to hear that news."

"Mr. Jared!" Tyler ran up and flung his arms around Jared's long legs before she could respond. "I'm glad you came to our party."

"Me, too." Shelly's eyes misted when Jared reached down to include her son in their embrace. "It's good to see you."

"Want some ice cream? We have three flavors."

"Neapolitan," she explained when Jared looked confused. "Chocolate, vanilla, and strawberry. Three flavors in one."

"Sounds good," Jared agreed.

"First, you have to put on your party hat." Shelly plopped a bright blue hat on his head, thinking his eyes were a much prettier blue. "And here's your noisemaker."

Jared blew it loudly, then smiled. She was touched at how Jared played along as they stuffed themselves with ice cream and leftover tacos.

Finally, the hour grew late enough for Ty to go to bed.

Shelly was thrilled that Jared didn't make up an excuse to leave. He'd mentioned wanting to talk, but she was hoping maybe he'd kiss her again.

She'd learned something amazing today. Exciting news was a hundred times better when you had someone to share it with. And if the unthinkable had happened, if she'd been given bad news, then maybe she would have dealt with it better if she'd had Jared with her.

Maybe, just maybe, she didn't have to do everything alone.

"I'll just be a few minutes," she said, following Tyler toward his room.

"I know." Jared leaned down to pick up the dirty dishes. "I'll be here."

"I know." She flashed an impish grin. Ty dawdled in the bathroom, then again when he wanted a bedtime story. Shelly leaned down and firmly kissed his cheek.

"I love you, Ty, but I'll read you two stories tomorrow, okay? I have to clean up the party mess, remember?" Flimsy excuse, maybe, but she knew he was tired enough to fall asleep soon.

"Okay." He yawned and snuggled down into the covers. "G'night." Then his eyes popped open. "Almost forgot to say my prayers."

Shelly tried to be patient as Ty went through his nightly ritual. She smiled when he once again added Jared to his prayer list.

True to his word, Jared was in the process of cleaning away the mess.

"Leave them, I'll take care of it later."

Jared turned from the sink to face her, his intense gaze making her catch her breath. "You shouldn't have to clean up everything alone."

"I'm not alone." And she'd never been so happy to admit it. "You're here. Have I told you how happy I am to see you?"

His blue eyes darkened when she approached. He stared at her mouth as if completely fascinated. "No, I, uh, don't think you did."

She couldn't help but smile. This uncertain side of Jared was fun to tease. She stepped closer and reached up to rest her hand in the center of his chest. "Dishes later."

He gave a bemused nod. "I, uh, we need to talk."

"Later," she repeated. She slipped her arms around his neck and reached up to press her mouth against his, kissing him the way she'd longed to do since experiencing his embrace the first time.

10

J ared lost himself in Shelly's arms, her kiss robbing him of all conscious thought. If he'd thought their previous kiss was hot, this one was scorching. It was as if she'd thrown all her reservations into the wind, allowing the breeze to carry them away.

He never wanted the kiss to end, but the incessant ringing of his cell phone eventually penetrated the cloud of desire surrounding them. With reluctance, he lifted his head, gulping oxygen as he tried to gather his scattered thoughts.

"Are you on call?" Shelly asked, leaning against him as if needing his support.

"No." Keeping one arm anchored around her waist, he dug his phone from his pocket. Seeing the number of his mother's cell phone on the screen made him wince. "Uh, sorry, but I need to take this."

She tipped her head back to look at him in confusion, then seemed to understand he needed his privacy. She stepped away from him, and he instantly wanted to draw her back, holding her close to his heart.

"Yeah?" He turned his back on Shelly and took a few steps away from her.

"Jared, what's going on? Your father and I have been waiting to hear from you. Have you made the necessary arrangements for us to see our grandson?"

"Uh, not yet." His mother's demanding tone brought a wave of guilt. He never should have joined in Shelly and Ty's celebration, shouldn't have kissed her like he was starving for the barest taste of her. Not when she still didn't know what he'd come to talk to her about.

"Why not? What's taking so long?" His mother sounded more than a little annoyed, and he understood they'd been waiting since their arrival earlier today for him to speak with Shelly. "You promised we'd get to see him soon. Your father agreed to wait on flying, but it's all I can do to keep him grounded. The sooner you make the arrangements for us to see the boy, the better."

He glanced over to where Shelly stood, her arms wrapped tightly around her as if she were already regretting their kiss. An embrace she'd initiated. "This isn't a good time. I'll call you back, okay?"

"Jared, wait . . ."

But he ignored her, disconnecting from the call. As much as he needed to talk to Shelly, he wasn't sure confessing what he'd done was something he needed to tell her right now. Not when she was still celebrating the fact that Ty's testing had come back normal.

"Mommy?" Ty's voice cut through the silence that hung between them. "My tummy hurts."

"Too much ice cream," she said on a sigh. "Listen, Jared, I need to take care of Tyler. This, uh, well, never mind. We can, uh, talk tomorrow."

"Sure." He understood she was already regretting their

kiss but couldn't figure out why. What had changed in the few minutes between his cell phone ringing and now? Other than Tyler's stomachache. "Listen, Shelly, will you and Tyler have dinner with me tomorrow? I really do want to talk."

"I'm not sure that's a good idea." She took a step backward, putting distance between them. "There isn't anything to talk about."

There certainly was, but this wasn't the time. He wanted nothing more than to kiss her again, but he forced himself to stay where he was, pinning her with a determined gaze.

"Six o'clock. Dinner. Tomorrow. Both you and Ty better be ready." With that, he turned and left.

Outside in his car, he slid behind the wheel and sat for a long moment. His phone rang again, but he ignored it. The easy part of this mess was convincing his parents that he needed time to spring the truth on Shelly. The longer he could keep them in Boston, the better.

The hard part would be to admit to Shelly what he'd done. How he'd pried into her personal life.

Something he should have done before he'd kissed her senseless.

At this point, he could only hope and pray she'd forgive him.

SHELLY WENT to Ty's room and pulled him into her arms. Stupid to have given him so much ice cream, regardless of their celebration. She gave him something to settle his stomach, then held him until he fell back to sleep.

Creeping from his room, she returned to the kitchen. Embarrassing to think about how she'd thrown herself at Jared, the man she worked with on a regular basis. What was wrong with her? Even if she was ready to move on, the reasons she'd avoided relationships until now remained the same. Okay, maybe Ty wasn't looking at a future that included dialysis or a kidney transplant, but that didn't mean she wanted the little boy to get hurt if a relationship didn't work out.

And working together was probably the quickest way to destroy a potential relationship.

Knowing she wouldn't sleep, she busied herself with cleaning up the mess in the kitchen. Who was the woman who'd called Jared? She hadn't meant to eavesdrop, but in the few seconds before he'd moved away, she'd heard a shrill female voice. The way Jared had turned away from her was also an indication that he didn't want her to overhear the conversation.

A former girlfriend? Wife? Now that she thought about it, she didn't know that much about Jared's personal life. Other than his father was sick with heart failure. But he could have been engaged, married, or seeing someone else before moving here to Milwaukee.

A kernel of jealousy invaded her mind before she could squash it like a bug. Enough. She had a son, so what if Jared had someone else in his life? He didn't seem like the kind of guy who would kiss her while seeing someone else, but some men didn't consider a kiss a big deal. For all she knew, he could have a slew of women on the side.

When the kitchen was spotless, she crawled into bed. Hours later, after a restless night's sleep, she got up to make Tyler breakfast. Knowing that her son was healthy helped to push thoughts of Jared out of her mind.

This was all she'd wanted. All she needed. A healthy son meant everything to her.

"I'm hungry," Tyler announced, entering the kitchen.

"What would you like?" She mentally reviewed the contents of her fridge. "I think we have eggs and bacon."

"I love bacon," Ty said reverently.

"You love people, not food," she corrected.

"I love you, Mommy. And Mr. Jared."

That gave her pause, understanding this was exactly what she was trying to protect Tyler from. No way was she going to dinner with Jared tonight. This had to end, now. Before her son became even more attached to him. "I love you, too." She pulled a carton of eggs out of the fridge along with a half pound of bacon. "Brush your teeth and get dressed while I make breakfast, okay?"

"Okay." Ty dashed away to do as he was told.

Shelly cooked bacon and beat eggs, staying focused on the mundane tasks she had to get accomplished today. Considering she had to work tonight, which meant Ty would spend the night at Ellen's, leaving the chores until tomorrow wasn't an option.

When breakfast was finished, she did some laundry, then sat outside in a lawn chair while Ty amused himself on the tire swing suspended from the oak tree. Ellen's husband Jeff had hung it for her last year, and she appreciated having something for Tyler to do. Her lack of sleep caught up with her. Resting her head back against the frame of the chair, she closed her eyes, wishing Ty was still inclined to take naps. She could have used one herself.

Tired. She was so tired. Maybe she'd call Ellen and see if she'd be willing to have Ty come over earlier so she could get a decent nap in. After the last time Jared had threatened to take her off duty, she didn't want to show up for her shift exhausted. Her mind floated in a blissful state of drowsy relaxation . . .

Crack!

The sound, similar to that of a gunshot, had her bolting up from her chair. Too late. Her eyes widened with horror as she watched Tyler fall.

"Mo-om!" His terrified scream split the air, and she could have sworn his tiny body bounced as he hit the ground beneath the old oak tree with a horrible *thunk*. It took her a precious moment to realize her son had been trying to climb up the rope when the branch holding the suspended tire swing had broken.

"Tyler." She fell to her knees at his side, raising her voice so he could hear her above his crying. "It's okay, I'm here." Her hands cradled his head, her gaze raking him for signs of injury. No blood, but that wasn't necessarily reassuring as he could be bleeding on the inside.

"Hurts, it hurts," he sobbed as she struggled to prevent him from moving too much.

"What hurts, Ty?" She gently, very gently, log-rolled him onto his back, running a hand down the length of one leg, then the other. That's when she saw it, the abnormal bend to his left arm.

"My arm hurts," he cried.

"Don't move." She planted her hand on the center of his chest to keep him still. "Stay right here. I'm going to call for help. Don't move or it will hurt worse, okay?"

He nodded tearfully, and she could have kicked herself for leaving her phone inside the house. A tactic to avoid talking to Jared if he attempted to call.

"Stay still," she repeated. Satisfied that he'd listen, Shelly took precious seconds to sprint into the house to grab her cell phone before hurrying back outside. She dialed 911, requesting an ambulance and giving her address as she returned to Ty.

Feeling slightly better knowing help was on the way, she

knelt beside Ty and gently assessed him for other signs of injury. "It's okay, sweetie. The ambulance will be here soon. We'll get your arm fixed in no time."

Tyler's sobs quieted as she continued speaking softly and reassuringly to him. When the paramedics arrived, they were wonderful, cradling Ty's broken arm while lifting him carefully into the ambulance. Hearing she was a nurse, they allowed her to ride along, which she did without hesitation, uncaring how she'd get back home.

In the emergency department of Children's Memorial, the hospital staff recognized her and helped get Tyler settled. The place was busy, the antiseptic scent sharp as the air around her was filled with crying, wailing kids of various ages. It all seemed surreal to be in the ER as a patient. While they waited for the orthopedic specialist to arrive, Shelly closed her eyes and fought the insane urge to call Jared.

Then it hit her. She'd have to call him, or at least call Lifeline. For the second time in two weeks, she'd have to call off work. On a Saturday night, no less. She felt so guilty but knew that the sooner she called, the sooner they could find a replacement.

When she heard Jared's deep voice on the other end of the line, she almost dropped her phone. "Jared, this is Shelly. Listen, I'm really sorry, but I'm not going to make my shift tonight. I'm in the Children's Memorial Emergency Department with Ty."

"What happened?" His sharp question pierced her ear.

"He'll be okay, I think, but he fell from the tire swing in our backyard and broke his arm." She was pleased that she sounded calm and rational. "I really feel terrible about calling in again. This isn't a habit of mine; I'm normally very reliable."

"Don't worry about it, we'll get someone to cover your shift. I'll be right there."

"Oh, that's not necessary—" She stopped when she realized she was talking to dead air. Jared had already disconnected from the line. She frowned as she shoved her phone into her pocket. It was sweet that he wanted to be there for Ty, but she knew that would only cause her son to bond with him more than he already had.

Jared showed up in Tyler's cubicle fifteen minutes later. "Grace is going to work your shift tonight," he said before turning toward Ty. "Hey, slugger, how are you?" He placed a hand on Ty's shoulder. "Broke your arm, huh?"

"Yeah. I tried to climb up the rope and falled down." Tyler's lower lip trembled. "I knew I wasn't supposed to climb the rope, but Mom was resting her eyes, so she didn't see me."

Shelly's cheeks flushed with guilt. She wouldn't have been resting her eyes if she hadn't lost sleep over Jared in the first place.

Her issues weren't Ty's fault. Yet, he'd been the one to pay the price for her inattentiveness.

"Have they taken X-rays yet?" Jared asked.

"Yes, we're waiting to see the orthopedic surgeon." She avoided his direct gaze. "It's broken, but I'm fairly sure that calling the ortho team is a little overkill. I'm sure he'll get a cast and be just fine."

"Ms. Bennett?" A youthful-looking resident poked his head into the cube. "Dr. Graves will be here in a few minutes, he's reviewing your son's X-rays now."

"Great." Shelly smiled. When an older-looking gentleman walked in, with salt-and-pepper hair, she immediately felt reassured. She knew residents needed to learn, but she would rather talk to the specialist herself.

"I'm Matt Graves." He shook her hand as he introduced himself. He gave Jared a nod, then earned more brownie points when he addressed her son. "Hi, Tyler. I understand you fell and broke your arm?"

"I was climbing the rope," Ty admitted solemnly. He'd stopped crying, but his cheeks were still damp from his tears. "The tree branch broke, and I fell."

"I see." Dr. Graves gently examined Ty's swollen arm. "You did a good job breaking it, that's for sure." He turned back to face Shelly. "He has a compound fracture of both the radius and ulna bones. He's going to need surgery, and while I normally like to wait for the swelling to go down, his fracture needs to be stabilized immediately. I'd like to operate tonight, if possible. I'll need you to sign a consent form for the surgery and for giving him blood."

"Surgery tonight? Blood?" she repeated with a squeak of alarm. The room spun as the surgeon's words registered in her brain.

"There are risks to surgery and to receiving blood," Dr. Graves continued. "Our blood bank screens every unit of blood very carefully, but there is still always a risk of hepatitis, HIV..."

"I know the risks," Shelly interrupted. "I'm a pediatric nurse for Lifeline."

His expression softened. "Since there's time, you could donate a unit of blood for him yourself if that would make you feel better."

Tears sprang to her eyes, and she blinked them away rapidly. "I would, but I can't. Tyler has O-negative blood. I'm A-negative." Inwardly, she wanted to scream in frustration. Granted, getting blood wasn't nearly as dangerous as it used to be with all the testing they do now, but as Dr. Graves said, there's always a risk.

Back when she'd been afraid Ty would need a transplant, she'd known she wouldn't be able to donate a kidney for him. Now she couldn't even donate a simple unit of blood.

"I can donate blood for Ty." Jared's voice cut through her thoughts.

"You can?" She stared at him in surprise.

"Yes." He met her gaze dead-on. "My blood type is O-negative, too. In fact"—he paused, cleared his throat, and took a step toward her—"everyone in my family has O-negative blood. Me, my parents, and my brother, Mark. I know this is a bad time to tell you this, but I know who you are, Shelly. I know your real name is Sharon Leigh Wilson. And I also know that Tyler is Mark's son."

11

"No." She didn't want to believe what Jared had just said. She shook her head in an effort to dislodge the giant bumblebee that buzzed in her ears. "I—no. You can't be related."

"It's true. I'm sorry to tell you like this, but I'm not sorry we found you. We've been looking for you and Ty since you left six years ago."

"Ms. Bennett?" Dr. Graves sounded a bit impatient with their unrelated discussion. "Are you giving consent for your son to have surgery or not?"

"Yes." Grateful, she turned her attention to the important issue at hand. Should she take a chance on using blood from the blood bank for Ty? No, she couldn't do it. There was no sense in taking the risk. Not when there was another viable option. "If Jared, er, Dr. O'Connor will donate blood."

"I'll head over to the blood bank right now," Jared offered.

"They're not open this late on a Saturday," Dr. Graves warned. "You can try the lab, but they don't like to do this sort of thing on a rushed basis."

"They'll do it." Jared's tone was firm. "I'll pull whatever strings necessary to make it happen."

She took note of the steely determination in Jared's eyes before he turned and left.

"Fine, I'll call in the OR team." Dr. Graves nodded at her and Ty, then followed Jared out of the cubicle.

Alone, Shelly stared at her son. His face was pale against his thick, dark brown hair. And there in the corners of his eyes were the tiny crinkles that were so much like his father's.

She'd always known how much Ty looked like Mark. She swallowed hard, trying to prevent the sick feeling in her stomach from violently erupting. After all these years, Mark's family had found her. Jared was Mark's brother. He knew her real name.

Jared was Ty's uncle.

Her knees gave away, and she collapsed in a nearby chair as the magnitude of what she'd recently learned hit hard. She hadn't even considered the meaning behind what Jared had just told her. They'd searched for her and for Ty over the past six years.

They wanted her son. Just like when they'd tried to buy him from her before he was born. *They wanted her son!*

"Mommy? My arm hurts."

Shelly used every last shred of strength she had to pull herself together. There would be time to deal with Jared later. Right now, her son needed her. She stood and used Ty's call button to ring for the nurse. "I know, sweetie. We'll see if they can give you something to make the pain better."

"Okay." Ty's lower lip trembled. "It hurts really bad. Will the surgery hurt really bad, too?"

"The doctor will put you to sleep for the surgery, but when you wake up, there might be some pain. But you'll get pain medicine afterward, too. Everything is going to be fine, Ty. I'll be here with you the whole time."

The nurse brought in some non-narcotic pain medicine and injected it into Ty's IV. Shortly thereafter, the pediatric anesthesiologist came into the room to review Ty's health history. He dutifully noted Ty's recent bladder infections and the results of his even more recent testing.

"What about blood?" the anesthesiologist asked. "I always try hard to avoid blood transfusions, but depending on how things go, I may not have a choice."

"I know. Jared, I mean, Dr. O'Connor is donating some for him right now. He's O-neg just like Tyler."

"That's fine. I'll make a note to use donor-directed blood. Although, you know the blood bank isn't keen on that process."

"I'd really like you to use Dr. O'Connor's blood if you need it," she insisted.

"Got it." He made another notation on his scrap of paper, then took out his stethoscope. She was impressed with the way he unclipped the small panda bear hanging from the tubing and showed it to Ty before placing the cold instrument on his chest. "This is Paddy the panda. He likes visiting kids like you."

Despite the pain, Ty smiled at the small toy, especially when the anesthesiologist clipped it to Ty's index finger. "Hey, I think Paddy likes you." He smiled reassuringly at Ty as he listened to his heart and lungs. When he finished, he put the stethoscope away. "You're going to have a cool cast on your arm. All the kids at your school will get to sign their names on it. Pretty neat, huh?"

Ty's grin was weak, but Shelly could tell he was cheered up by the idea.

Within two hours, the hospital staff had everything

ready for Ty's surgery. Jared had succeeded in pulling strings to get his blood donated for Ty and sent up to the OR. The two of them walked alongside Ty's gurney as the ED staff wheeled him toward the operating room. At the door, Shelly leaned over to give Ty a hug and kiss.

"I love you," she whispered against his ear. "You're going to be fine. I'll be waiting right here for you, I promise."

Drowsy from the medication he'd been given, Ty nodded. "I love you, too, Mommy."

When Shelly stepped away, Jared took his turn. "Hey, Ty, I'll take care of your mom while you're gone, okay?"

"Will you be here when I come out?" Ty asked.

"Absolutely. I'll be here with your mom, waiting for you." She was surprised when Jared leaned down to drop a kiss on the top of Ty's head. His voice was thick with emotion as he added, "See you soon."

Ty nodded, his eyes sliding closed.

Shelly stood for several long moments after Tyler had disappeared into the sterile section of the operating room. Her vision blurred with tears, and she swiped them away, wishing she'd brought a tissue.

"He'll be fine." Jared wrapped his arm around her shoulders.

For a moment she allowed herself the luxury of leaning against him, absorbing his strength. Ty had looked so brave. She hoped and prayed the surgery would be completed without any difficulty.

After a moment, she pulled away, reminding herself who Jared was and what he wanted. "There's a waiting area around the corner."

"Let's go." Jared followed her over and sat down across from her. "Look, Shelly—"

"Wait." She held up a hand to stop him. "I need to know

just one thing. How long? How long have you known my real identity?"

The flash of hesitation confirmed her worst fears. "Since Thursday morning, after our Lifeline shift."

Two days? She felt sick at knowing they'd danced and celebrated Ty's health, that she'd thrown herself into his arms and kissed the daylights out of him. All the while he'd known the truth. She went hot and cold in the space of a heartbeat.

"I can't believe it." Her voice was hoarse, and she wanted to crawl under the chair to get away from him.

"Shelly, don't. I had so much fun celebrating with you and Ty Friday night, and I'm lucky I was able to share that moment with you." Jared reached out to take her hand, but she snatched it away, despite the shards of longing that accompanied his familiar touch.

"Don't. How could you kiss me like that without telling me the truth? Was that your way of softening me up? Did you think that if we became close that I'd be willing to allow you into Ty's life?"

"Of course not!" His denial rang true, but she didn't want to believe it. "I've been attracted to you from the moment we first met. I kissed you the first time without knowing who you really were. Don't tell me you didn't feel the same way. Can't you see? These feelings between us started long before I uncovered the truth."

"I'm not sure I believe that." Unable to maintain her anger and frustration, she let out a sigh and turned away. "But I guess I was the one to initiate our last kiss, wasn't I?"

"Shelly, please. Don't do this. Don't taint something beautiful with your anger."

She shook her head, staring sightlessly out through the window. There was a maple tree in the distance, the green leaves beginning to turn yellow. Autumn was normally her favorite time of year. But she found no joy in the bright colors. "I didn't even know Mark had a brother until that night. The night I told him I was pregnant."

She sensed Jared coming up to stand behind her. She tensed, but he didn't touch her or interrupt.

Closing her eyes, she remembered that fateful night. "I probably shouldn't have sprung the news on him like I did, but I was upset myself and not thinking clearly. It wasn't just finding out I was pregnant, but the timing was terrible. I only had two more semesters of school to finish before graduating with my bachelor's degree in nursing. I wasn't sure how I would handle everything I needed to do."

"Was Mark supportive?" Jared asked.

"Yes, but it didn't matter since later that same night he died in that terrible car crash." She thought about how devastated she'd been, suffering from nonstop morning sickness while reeling from the shock of losing Mark. "I think I went a little crazy for a while."

"Is that why you ran away?" Jared lightly stroked his hand down her back.

"No." His touch made her shiver, and she grew angry with herself for still responding to his nearness. "I ran because of your parents. I—just trust me on this. I couldn't stay. And you have to promise me that you won't tell them you found me. Found us." She turned to face him, grabbing his arm. "Promise me, Jared. I don't want your parents to know anything about me and Ty."

"Shelly, they already know." Jared said the words softly, but they felt as sharp as a knife. "They want to meet Ty."

"No! Absolutely not!" Panic sent her stumbling backward as if she could escape the inevitable. She struggled to breathe, to speak. "I won't let them see Ty. I won't! You can't force me to."

"Calm down, you're not being rational about this." Jared's expression was baffled by her reaction. "I don't understand. What's wrong with a set of grandparents wanting to see their grandson? Did they treat you badly? Did they look down on you for becoming pregnant? Or did they refuse to believe the baby was Mark's? What?"

"Worse. They tried to buy my baby." She stabbed him in the chest with her index finger, punctuating every word. "They offered me a million dollars to give up my son."

A MILLION DOLLARS? That was a lot of money, even for his well-to-do parents. So much money that Jared had trouble believing what Shelly was saying. "You must have misunderstood."

The harsh laugh that burst from her chest was anything but mirthful. "No. I didn't misunderstand. Your mother was quite clear on the terms. I get a million dollars and I give up all rights to my baby, staying out of his or her life forever. Take it or leave it." Her smile was brittle. "I left it."

Jared didn't know what to say. His mother's reaction since finding Shelly and Ty had been oddly intense, but this? He found it difficult to believe his parents honestly wanted custody of a five-year-old rambunctious boy. Not when his father's health was tenuous at best.

"Okay, listen, maybe they made the outrageous offer while crazed with grief. But you need to know, Shelly, they aren't a threat to you now. No one wants to take Ty away from you."

"Yeah, right." Shelly defensively crossed her arms across

her chest. "I don't believe that for a second. Your mother set the terms, but your father was the one who threw his legal clout into the bargain. He threatened to fight me for custody if I chose not to take their money. He claimed he could prove that a cocktail waitress"—she made air quotes with her fingers—"was an unfit mother."

Unfortunately, he could see his father making that kind of a rash statement. But five years ago, not now. Not when his health was so bad. "Shelly, please . . ."

"I don't care what you think, Jared. My answer is still no. I will not let them see Ty. End of discussion."

She turned and walked to the opposite side of the room as if she couldn't stand being near him. He let her go. Between Ty's traumatic injury, needing surgery, and finding out he knew her secret identity, she was too upset. He figured she'd reached the saturation point a long time ago. No sense in pushing things further. Ty wasn't in any condition to meet his grandparents anyway.

Speaking of which, Jared needed to call his parents to let them know about Ty's injury. He left the waiting area to walk down the hall, out of Shelly's earshot, then called his mother's cell phone. There was no answer, and the call instantly went straight to voice mail. He found that odd since she'd been badgering him incessantly over the past few days. When he tried his father's cell, that one went to voice mail, too.

With a frown, he slipped his phone back into his pocket. Where could his parents be on a Saturday afternoon that they both turned off their cell phones? Dinner and a movie? Didn't seem likely. If his father was feeling well enough, maybe they'd decided to go out.

Ten minutes later, his phone rang. It was his dad's number. "Hello? Dad?"

"Jared?" The connection wasn't great. "Can you hear me?"

"Barely." Jared hunched his shoulders and turned his back on the waiting room, lowering his voice. "Where are you?"

"We just landed at the airport in Chicago," his father said. "We have a short layover but will be in Milwaukee soon."

"No, don't tell me you're coming to see Ty. I told you to wait till I called."

"We got tired of waiting. It's been six years; we want to meet our grandson. We'll be landing in Milwaukee in about an hour. Be there to pick us up."

Not possible. Jared promised to be here when Ty came out of surgery, so as far as he was concerned, his parents would have to wing it. "I can't pick you up. Take a cab and find a hotel. I'll get in touch with you later."

"What do you mean you can't pick us up?" His father sounded outraged. "Aren't you the director of that helicopter place? I'm sure you can spare a little time to pick us up."

He ground his teeth in an effort to hold on to his temper. "That's not the point. You didn't tell me you were flying out here today and I'm not rearranging my life for your impulsive behavior. Take a cab, find a hotel near the airport, and I'll call you later."

Jared disconnected from the call before his father could continue arguing. Then he turned his phone off so they couldn't keep calling to hound him. With a sigh, he rubbed his jaw. Maybe Shelly had a point about his parents. He was used to their stubbornness, but he could see how a young pregnant woman would be intimidated by them. He and Mark had sometimes felt the same way, Mark more so than him. He'd always wanted to be a doctor, which meant the pressure was on his brother to follow in their father's foot-steps to become a lawyer.

Poor Mark hadn't been thrilled with the idea but had given studying law a try, allowing himself to be sucked into their father's master plan.

His fault. Everything came back down to the fact that Mark's death was his fault. If they hadn't argued about Shelly and the baby, Mark would still be alive and Shelly wouldn't have felt the need to run halfway across the country. If Jared had agreed to go to law school, the pressure would have been off Mark entirely. His brother could have chosen a different path, maybe even becoming the writer he'd dreamed of being. But Jared hadn't really known how unhappy Mark had been until the night of his death.

"I'm getting married, Jared. Congratulate me! I'm going to be a husband and a father."

"Married? A father? Are you crazy? You're still in school. How can you afford to get married?"

"I'm dropping out. I never wanted to be a lawyer, and I detest law school. Why do you think I hang out so much at Stephan's? Not that I can complain, since going to Stephan's helped me meet Leigh. And she thinks I should follow my dream of becoming an author. She loves my writing, and you know what? That's exactly what I'm going to do. I don't care what our old man says. Let him cut me out of his will. I don't want his stupid money anyway."

"Look, drop out of school if that's what you want to do. It makes sense anyway, you'll need to work with a baby to support. But getting married? Focusing on your writing? That's crazy. Do you even love her?"

"Yeah, I love her or I wouldn't have proposed. Besides, I refuse to leave Leigh high and dry with a baby to raise. I'm gonna marry her, don't try to talk me out of it."

"Listen, Mark, take a breath. Supporting the baby is your responsibility, and you can help Leigh without marrying her. But you'll need a job to do that. A paying job. Writing is a dream, but you need to face reality. Don't do something rash that you'll regret later."

"You're a jerk, Jared, you know that? I'm going to quit school and get married. With or without your brotherly support."

Mark had stormed out the door, crashing his car into the concrete median less than ten miles from Jared's apartment.

Of course, in hindsight, Jared had suspected that some of his brother's comments could have been the alcohol talking, especially upon discovering in the final autopsy results that Mark's blood alcohol level was twice the legal limit. He should have known Mark was drinking and dropped the whole subject from the start.

Guilt had been his constant companion ever since that fateful night. Jared knew if Mark were still alive, he'd be the one here at the hospital, comforting Shelly. Mark and Shelly would be married, possibly already having had a second child, this one a girl with her mother's big green eyes and chocolate-brown hair. Jealousy nipped at the back of his neck. Was he going nuts? How could he be envious of his dead brother?

Easy. Because Shelly loved Mark. Had created a beautiful child with him. Would still be with him if Jared hadn't goaded his brother into driving under the influence.

He forced himself to admit the truth. He was jealous of the love Shelly and Mark had shared. Knowing Shelly's Wonder Woman tendencies, he knew she would have fought hard to make the marriage work. Not like so many others who threw in the towel when they hit the first storm at sea. Wonder Woman wouldn't have let any storm separate her from her man.

Or her son.

Jared turned back toward the waiting area with a deep ache in his heart. He watched as Shelly nervously paced the small length of the room. Mark might be dead, but his essence lived on in Jared's guilt. All he could do was to somehow make it up to Shelly and Ty.

Starting with mending the rift between Shelly and his parents.

12

"**M**s. Bennett?"

Jared noticed how Shelly leaped to her feet, eyeing the weary-looking surgeon that entered the room. He understood her anxiety and rose to stand beside her.

"Yes?" Her voice held a note of panic.

"Your son's surgery went fine," Dr. Graves informed her. "I had to place hardware in his arm, so don't freak out when you see the pins sticking out of his bones."

She visibly gulped. "How many pins?"

"Four." He identified the places on his forearm where he'd placed the pins. "The contraption looks much worse than it is, and the nurses will do their best to keep Tyler comfortable."

"When can she see him?" Jared asked.

"He'll be sedated for a while yet, but I've informed the post-anesthesia recovery nurses that you'd insist on coming in. As a nurse, I'm inclined to give you that permission. But only for a few minutes." His brow puckered. "You know rest is critical to recovery."

"I won't be a bother," Shelly assured him.

"How long do you anticipate keeping him here in the hospital?" Jared knew there was a push to get patients out of the hospital sooner, rather than later, but with the pins Graves had placed, he figured they were looking at one overnight stay, maybe two. Shelly was already bone weary, and there was still a long road of recovery ahead.

"We'll see how it goes, but with Shelly being a nurse, I'm fairly certain we'll be able to send him home in a couple of days."

"Thank you, Dr. Graves." Shelly clasped the doctor's hand fervently. "For everything."

The surgeon smiled. "You're welcome. The post-anesthesia recovery area is through those double doors."

Shelly nodded and turned to Jared. Despite their earlier argument, the long waiting had eventually worn her down. She was talking to him again, and he was glad she indicated he could come along.

"After you," he said, gesturing toward the PACU.

The area was a bustle of activity, even on a Saturday evening. When they walked in, a nurse glanced up and waved them over. Although he and Shelly both knew what to expect, seeing Ty so tiny and frail against the stark white sheets deeply bothered him. The little boy was so young, facing the surgery with courage and bravery.

"Ty? Mommy's here."

The boy opened his eyes in response to Shelly calling his name, but his unfocused gaze convinced Jared that he was still feeling the impact of anesthesia.

"We'll stay close by," Jared told the boy. But this time, Ty didn't open his eyes or acknowledge that he'd heard.

They didn't stay long, especially knowing they were in

the nurse's way. She promised to call them as soon as Tyler was assigned a room, so they could meet him there.

Back in the waiting room, Jared glanced at his watch. Did he have time to meet with his parents to fill them in on what was going on? He wanted to be there when Tyler woke up, but by the looks of how groggy he'd been, Jared knew it could take several hours before the little boy knew they were there.

Best to do it now, rather than later, he decided. He turned to Shelly. "I have a quick errand to run." He wasn't about to tell her that his parents had impulsively decided to arrive in town. The last thing she needed was that added stress on top of everything else. "I'll be back in an hour. Will you be okay here while I'm gone?"

"Sure." Her smile didn't reach her eyes. "I've been a single mother for a long time, Jared. I can handle it fine without you."

Ouch. Hearing her boldly tell him she didn't need him any more hurt, more than it should. She clearly hadn't gotten over his request to allow Ty to meet his grandparents, and at this rate, it might be best to convince his parents to turn around and head back to Boston.

He wished once again that he could turn back the clock, returning to the time she'd taken him into her arms and kissed him. Logically, he knew it was impossible, and he did his best to ignore the stab of longing.

"You have my cell number, right?" It was a rhetorical question, and he knew it. "Please, Shelly. Please call me if you need anything. Or if they bring him out of the PACU earlier than expected. I want to be here for him. I don't want to break my promise."

"Then maybe you shouldn't go." Shelly looked at him

expectantly, as if waiting to hear what errand was so important.

His determination to leave wavered. Was this Shelly's way of asking him to stay? Did he really need to go meet his parents? One more glance at Shelly's closed facial expression convinced him. Yes, he needed to go. Surely once he explained the situation, his parents would relax their all-fired mission to meet their grandson.

He needed to buy a little time. A few days. Long enough for Shelly to have cooled down for a rational conversation. When he reminded her of his father's health issues, she'd have to understand his need to see his grandson before he died.

"I'll be back in an hour," he repeated. Then he turned and left.

HIS PARENTS WEREN'T hard to find. They'd ignored his instructions to stay near the airport, choosing a very nice hotel close to his condo. He should have figured that's what they'd do.

"Where is our grandson?" His mother's demanding tone made him scowl.

"Sit down, Mom. Dad." His authoritative tone must have gotten through because his parents sank down onto the sofa in their suite. "Ty broke his arm when he fell out of a tree this morning. He's already gone through surgery. The doctor had to place four pins in his arm to keep his bones stabilized. He's fine," he added quickly when his parents' faces registered frank alarm. "But he's not up to having visitors, especially from grandparents he doesn't even know about. And frankly, neither is Shelly."

His mother sniffed. "What kind of mother lets her son climb a tree?"

Jared shot her a narrow look. "Knock it off. Don't you dare go there. Shelly is a wonderful mother. She also holds the key to allowing you to see Ty. Don't you think it would be better to think of ways to get on her good side rather than insulting her parenting abilities?"

"Hrmph." His father had more color in his cheeks than he'd noticed the last time they were together. Maybe news of finding Ty had given him a boost. "We have the law on our side. There's plenty of case law to support our rights as grandparents. We can sue for visitation rights."

Jared wanted to rail at them to knock it off but managed to hold his tongue. Swallowing hard, he decided to try another tactic. "Think about what you're saying," he begged. "Shelly and Ty have been doing very well on their own, without you. Without any of us. Creating animosity, especially by pulling cheap lawyer tactics, isn't going to help."

"Cheap!" His mother jumped to her feet and planted her hands on her hips. "She's the cheap waitress who took off, denying us the ability to be a part of our only grandchild's life!"

"And why is that, Mom? What exactly did you say that made Shelly run?"

She flushed and sank back down onto the sofa. With one hand she smoothed the wrinkles in her slacks. "I—we were afraid she'd do something crazy after finding out that Mark was dead. She was a cocktail waitress! All we wanted was the chance to give Mark's son a secure future. The life he deserved. We didn't mean to scare her off."

"Yeah, because any woman would jump at the chance to get a million dollars, right?"

His mother dropped her gaze. "I just thought . . ." She didn't finish.

Jared's anger dissipated. As much as he wanted to blame his parents for their ridiculous behavior, he knew that none of this would have happened if he hadn't argued with Mark in the first place. He should have supported his brother, instead of calling him nuts for wanting to follow his dream.

The fault solely rested with him. Not his parents.

"Well, you did scare her away. So you need to trust me when I tell you this isn't a good time. Shelly doesn't have one iota of faith in your intentions, and she's not a cocktail waitress anymore. She's a flight nurse. Telling her the law is on your side is a sure way to eliminate any chance you might have of meeting your grandson."

His parents didn't concede, the familiar stubborn glint in their eyes making him groan. What part of this didn't they understand?

"Don't we all want what's best for Ty?" He looked between the two of them until they nodded. "I know Shelly. Once she understands that meeting you would be good for Ty, she'll come around. We need to give her a little time."

"Time? Bah." His father waved a hand, his expression grumpy as he rubbed a hand subconsciously over his chest. "I don't have time. Who knows when this ticker of mine will give out for good?"

"Joe, don't say things like that," his mother admonished. She put her arm around his shoulders.

"Dad, you flew here on your own free will, against your doctor's orders, I might add. I don't think a few more days will hurt." Although Jared could relate to his father's concern, he wasn't going to budge on this. "I'll be in touch with you tomorrow. For now, I'm heading back to the hospital." He moved toward the door.

"Wait! When tomorrow?" His mother clearly didn't want to let him go.

"I'm not sure. Sometime tomorrow morning." He glanced over his shoulder. "I'll call you to let you know how Ty is doing, okay?"

"All right," his mother agreed.

On arriving at the hospital, he headed straight to the waiting room where he'd left Shelly. His timing was perfect because they were just wheeling Ty down the hall in a gurney. Shelly walked beside them, barely glancing at him, her gaze riveted on her son.

"Hey, Ty," he greeted the boy.

"You're here." Ty's pinched face lit up.

"You bet. And I'm sticking around to see that you get better soon." Jared noticed Ty's left arm was propped up on a pillow, four metal pins sticking out of his tiny arm attached to a stabilizing bar. He ached to ease the child's discomfort and hoped that his being there helped a little.

Once they had Ty settled in his room, Shelly made herself comfortable in the lounge chair next to his bed. He took the hard-backed chair, knowing she needed the rest more than he did.

"So what's going on at Lifeline?"

He looked surprised for a moment, then realized she assumed his errand was work related.

"I didn't go to Lifeline." He couldn't lie to her, not with everything that had happened over the past twenty-four hours. He pulled his chair closer so their talking wouldn't disturb Ty. He stared down at his clasped hands for a moment, then met her gaze. "I won't lie to you, Shelly. I spoke to my parents to let them know what happened to Ty."

"You what?" Her voice was a low furious hiss. "You're

giving them updates? Hourly reports?" The biting sarcasm didn't suit her. "Have you told them about Ty's bladder infections and his kidney tests, too?"

"No. Shelly, please, don't do this. They care about Ty. I needed to explain things because they were getting impatient wanting to come and see him."

"Good. Because the answer is still no."

He sighed. She could teach stubbornness to a rhinoceros. "Would you please just—"

"No."

He clenched his jaw and let it go. The more he pressed, the more she'd dig in her heels. His parents treated her terribly, but that was six years ago. It wasn't healthy to hang on to this level of anger for that long. "I'd like to stay with you for a while, if you don't mind."

"You can do whatever you like, I don't care."

Her words cut deep. Jared tried to convince himself that she didn't really mean it, but deep down, he suspected she did. Years of distrust wasn't going to evaporate overnight. Somehow, he needed to find a way to convince her that his parents wouldn't do anything to hurt their grandson.

Or rather, that he wouldn't allow his parents to do anything to hurt Ty. He was on her side in this. Hers and Tyler's.

If only he could find a way to convince her.

JARED DIDN'T LEAVE EVEN though he sensed Shelly wished he would. The night was long with Ty waking every hour, whimpering in pain. Shelly instantly jumped up the moment he stirred, determined to meet his needs. She even took to assisting Ty with his medication, staying at his side, cradling him close while murmuring words of encouragement and comfort until the effects of the medicine kicked in.

His parents were wrong. Ty couldn't have a better mother than Shelly.

His presence was extraneous. He sat in the corner of Ty's room, out of the way while watching Shelly, mesmerized by her intensity as she cared for her son. She didn't need him, she had everything under control. He had no doubt that she would easily get through the next few days until Ty was truly on the mend.

Shelly would never know how he dreamed of their kiss. The way she'd stepped into his arms and wrapped her arms around his neck. What he wouldn't give to have that moment back again. To share the good times with her, as well as these difficult hours.

But there was no denying that was over. Shelly would never invite him back for a visit. Once he left the hospital, he'd only see her at work.

At least he had his memories.

By the time Dr. Graves came in to see Ty, Jared knew it was time to go. Although Shelly wasn't as cool to him as she'd been during the night, he was keenly aware of the fact that Tyler had no idea Jared was really his uncle. That his grandparents were so close, yet so far.

And nothing would change the fact that he wasn't Ty's father. He couldn't live Mark's life. No matter how much he cared about Shelly and Tyler.

"I need to get going," Jared said, rising to his feet after Dr. Graves left. "I hope you don't mind if I call in to check on Ty's progress."

"If you'd like," Shelly agreed.

There was so much more he wanted to say, but at that

moment the door to Ty's hospital room opened revealing his mother and father standing there.

"Hello, Ty." His mother boldly walked into the room, carrying an oversized stuffed animal in her arms. A giant teddy bear wearing a blue ribbon around his neck. His father came in behind his mother, grinning broadly.

Jared heard Shelly draw in a harsh breath.

"Hi." Ty looked at Jared's parents curiously, then shifted his gaze to the giant teddy bear. It was as if he wanted the bear but wasn't sure it was meant for him. "Who are you?"

Jared's mother beamed, her eyes suspiciously moist as she stepped closer to Ty's bedside, apparently oblivious to the twin green daggers Shelly was shooting in her direction. "I'm your grandma, and this is your grandpa. Ty, your daddy was our son."

13

G*et out! Get out! Get out!* The silent screams echoed in Shelly's head but remained locked within her tight throat. She gripped the side rail on Ty's bed with white knuckles, hardly able to comprehend what was happening.

It was like watching a freight train barreling toward her precious son, yet unable to stop it. The teddy bear was a nice touch, she thought sarcastically. It would make her look small if she refused it as a gift for Ty.

She shot a venomous look at Jared. How could he have blatantly betrayed her wishes? Had he planned this little surprise visit all along? Was this why he'd asked to stay last night? Not for Ty's benefit or even hers as she'd hoped, but rather for his own personal agenda? That had to be exactly what he'd done.

How could she have misjudged Jared so badly?

"Is that for me?" Ty lifted his right hand toward the bear.

"Yes, of course." Elizabeth O'Connor bravely approached Ty's bed. "This is Billy the bear, and he wants you to get better soon."

It was all Shelly could do not to snatch the bear away and throw it back in Mark's mother's face. But she couldn't do that to Tyler.

And this was how it started, she thought helplessly. This is how the O'Connors would use their wealth to win Ty's love.

"I'm sorry," she interrupted, finally finding her voice. "But Ty isn't really up for visitors. If you could put the bear on the recliner on your way out, I'd appreciate it." She thought she did a good job of remaining polite when every instinct she possessed wanted to grab Ty and to run.

To another state. Far away from Jared and his overbearing, obnoxious parents.

"We won't stay long." Joseph O'Connor stepped forward, forming a united front with his wife, silently challenging Shelly to physically throw them out. "After all these years, a few minutes won't hurt."

She narrowed her gaze, tightening her grip on the rail. Throwing Jared's parents out on their rear ends would be sweet, but Tyler shouldn't be a witness to such violence.

Especially from his mother.

"Are you really my grandma and grandpa?" Ty asked, his gaze swinging between the two of them.

"Yes, we really are." Elizabeth's expression softened as she turned toward Ty. Shelly nearly whimpered in distress. This couldn't be happening. Ty was her son. They couldn't take him away. She wouldn't stand for it! Why didn't they just go back to Boston where they belonged?

"Cool." Ty's eyelids drooped from the effects of the medication, but he fought the urge to sleep, forcing his eyes open. "It's Grandparents Day at school next week, and I didn't want a pretend one."

"A pretend one?" Elizabeth frowned and leaned closer. "What do you mean?"

"You know, there are some grandmas and grandpas that don't have grandkids of their own, so they come and pretend to be ours." His eyelids drooped again, and his words began to slur. "I'm glad to have my own . . ." His head rolled to the side as he succumbed to the effects of his pain medication.

Shelly's shoulders slumped as the implication of Ty's words sank deep. As much as she wanted to kick the O'Connors out, she hadn't known about Grandparents Day. Ty hadn't mentioned anything about it, until now.

"We'll be there, Ty, I promise." Elizabeth's voice broke, and she turned toward her husband who put a reassuring arm around her shoulders. "Did you hear that, Joe? Grandparents Day!"

"As you can see, Ty is exhausted and still suffering the effects of his surgery. He needs to rest." Shelly kept her voice firm, her eyes daring them to push. "Please leave."

"Mom, Dad, come with me." Jared spoke for the first time, his expression grim. "I'll take you back to the hotel."

"Oh, but—"

"Now." Jared's terse voice overrode his mother's protest. "You've seen Ty for yourself. That's what you came here for. Maybe you can see him again tomorrow."

Over my stone-cold dead body, Shelly thought. She watched as Joseph and Elizabeth tore themselves away from Ty's bedside with obvious reluctance, following Jared to the door.

Shelly took note of Jared's clenched jaw and smoldering gaze as he escorted them out. He was angry? With her? Seriously? What had he expected? That she'd welcome his parents with open arms? That she'd forgive his ultimate betrayal? Going behind her back to allow his parents to visit?

Not a chance. When the door closed behind them, Shelly's knees gave away, and she sank into the chair next to Ty's bed and buried her face in her hands, fighting tears. What should she do? What were her options? Running away had worked before, but it had been easier to do that before she had a nursing license. If she wanted to work as a nurse, she'd leave a paper trail a blind man could follow. But she didn't have to be a nurse. And she'd always wanted to see the West Coast . . .

No, she couldn't do it. She couldn't give up a career she loved or uproot Tyler to drag him across the country. He loved his school and the child care arrangements she had with Ellen. Alex was Ty's best friend.

Shelly lifted her head and swiped at her face. Her gaze landed on the stupid giant teddy bear. Billy the bear. The O'Connors had left it on the foot of Ty's bed. More proof they couldn't manage to do the smallest thing she asked of them.

But it was time to stop running and to face her past. She wasn't the scared kid she'd been when she'd gone to the O'Connors after Mark's death. She could hold her own, hire a lawyer if she had to.

The bottom line was that Ty wanted grandparents and not, she suspected, only because of Grandparents Day at school. How could she deny his desire for a family? Her parents had passed away when she was barely out of high school. Now Ty not only had doting grandparents, but he also had Uncle Jared. The man who'd wormed his way into their life. Who'd kissed and held her as if she were the only woman in the world. The man who'd traveled over a thousand miles just to find Ty.

The man who'd broken her heart.

Tears threatened again, and she brushed them away impatiently. What was done couldn't be undone, but she couldn't help thinking she would have been better off alone.

SHELLY COULDN'T BELIEVE Jared had the nerve to return to Ty's room ninety minutes after he and his parents had left. He caught her as she was leaving Ty's room to take a quick break while Ty was sleeping.

"I'm sorry."

"Don't even try to tell me that little scenario wasn't planned." Shelly wasn't in the mood to hear any more of his lies. Hadn't she been through enough already? "Just go away and leave us alone."

He nodded and held up his hands in a gesture of surrender. "If you want to believe that, then fine. I didn't plan it, but I can't say I'm completely sorry it happened this way. Now you can see for yourself my parents don't mean any harm. They just want to see their grandson."

"They want to buy him, you mean." Shelly didn't try to hide the bitterness in her tone. She walked down the hall, moving farther away from Ty's room. "The same way they tried to buy him before he was even born, six years ago."

"Shelly, wait." He lightly grasped her arm, but she quickly shook him off. "Don't let this animosity ruin what we have. Let's talk about this. Please?"

"Talk? About what?" Furious, she rounded on him. "About how you lied to me? How you did the one thing I asked you not to do? You used me to get to Ty."

"Don't be ridiculous." Jared stared at her. "I already told you, I fell for you long before I knew who you were."

"And I fell for you before I knew you were scum," she countered. "You and your parents want to see Ty? Fine. I'll agree to a few visits. On my schedule, not theirs. When it's good for Ty, not when they have a whim. But as far as ruining what we have? That's impossible because we don't have anything."

"You don't mean that." The anguish in his gaze tugged at her foolish heart.

"Yes, I do." She steeled her resolve. "There is nothing between us, Jared. And there never will be."

He was silent for a moment, so she turned and headed down the hall toward the elevators. Without glancing back, she knew Jared hadn't followed her. She told herself she was glad that he'd finally gotten the message through that thick skull of his.

As she stepped into the elevator to go down to the hospital cafeteria, she told herself she didn't need him. She didn't need anyone. She'd been doing just fine by herself over these past six years. This mess with Jared's parents only proved that she would have been better off if she hadn't met Jared O'Connor in the first place.

But the hollow knowledge formed a pit in her stomach, completely ruining her appetite.

ALONE ON THE following Monday morning, Jared sat in his office, staring blankly at the wall. The Lifeline crew was out on a flight, but the peace and quiet in the hangar didn't ease the torment in his heart.

Was this how desperate Mark had felt when he'd taken to going to Stephan's night after night, looking for something, anything to brighten his bleak future? Drinking wasn't the answer, but for the first time in years, Jared could understand why his brother may have gone down that route. Looking back, he should have realized Mark had developed a drinking problem, but he'd been too wrapped up in his own career to give much thought to his brother.

Until it had been too late.

He pressed the palms of his hands over his burning eyes. All the lives he'd saved as a physician, the way he'd found Shelly and Ty for his parents—nothing he'd done could erase his guilt over Mark's death. Why had he thought otherwise? Why should Shelly forgive him when he knew she was right? When he couldn't forgive himself? Not when he knew his actions had stolen Mark from her forever.

The urge to call Shelly was strong. He found himself wanting to call her, to talk to her every hour of every day.

A knock at his door interrupted his whirling thoughts. With a frown, he dropped his hands and called out, "Come in."

He couldn't have been more surprised when Shelly opened the door and entered the room. She didn't smile, but simply asked, "Do you have the schedule?"

"Huh?" Jared stared at her in surprise.

"You know, the flight schedule? I called earlier, but they said you were working on it. I need to figure out when I can return to work."

So she wasn't handing in her resignation, at least not yet. A nurse with Shelly's skills could get a job anywhere, and he figured it was only a matter of time. Even if they could manage to avoid each other most of the time, there was no guarantee they wouldn't end up flying together.

He glanced blankly at his desk, then noticed the corner of the schedule buried beneath a stack of paper. The schedule used to be built in the computer, but they'd had a few glitches, dangerous when you were depending on having a certain number of staff available to fly, so he'd gone back to paper temporarily while the IT guys tried to find a fix.

"You can take all the time you need," he said gruffly, handing it over. "I'll find a way to cover your shifts."

"I can't afford to be off much longer," Shelly informed him, staring with apparent fascination at the document in her hands. "My hot water heater went on the fritz. Ellen, my sitter, is with Ty right now. Dr. Graves is discharging him tomorrow, and Ellen is learning how to take care of his pins while I'm gone."

He soaked up the information about Ty, even though he'd secretly been calling and speaking to the surgeon each morning to find out Ty's progress for himself.

"Anyway, I think I can pick up some shifts starting on Wednesday, even though Tyler can't go back to school yet. Keeping him occupied at home will be the biggest challenge."

She studiously avoided his gaze, and Jared tried to think of something to say. Something to get her to keep talking. He'd happily buy her a new hot water heater if that was what was causing her financial crunch, but he knew she'd slap that offer right back into his face. He almost told her his parents would love to stay with Ty while she worked but bit his tongue before the words shot out of his mouth like a cannon. No doubt, Shelly would rather mud wrestle a five-hundred-pound gorilla than allow his parents to have any influence over her son.

"How's Ty feeling?" Jared asked, holding his breath and bracing himself for the inevitable brush-off.

"Better. His arm still hurts, but he's already figuring out how to manage tasks one-handed." She reached over and took a pen from Jared's desk, then proceeded to write her name on the schedule. "I see Kate requested to be off Wednesday and Thursday, so I'll take those shifts for her."

"I'll let her know." The conversation was uncomfortably stilted, but he couldn't find a way to ease the tension. Once, they had communicated like old friends.

But those days were gone.

Shelly set the schedule down. "Do you need anything else from me? Any paperwork?"

"No." He wanted to bring up Mark but wasn't sure how to approach the subject. "I, uh, need to tell you something about the night Mark died."

Shelly went tense, and he wondered if this would be the issue that would tip her over the edge, causing her to quit her job and leave for good. "What do you mean?"

"I've been living in guilt these past six years." This time, he was the one who avoided her gaze. "Mark came to me the night he found out you were pregnant. The night he proposed to you. He told me he was going to quit school, marry you, and write full time."

"He did?" She sounded surprised.

"We argued. I—" he swallowed hard, then continued, "I tried to talk him out of it."

"Why? He hated law school," Shelly interrupted. "That was just something he did to please your parents."

"Not that." He forced himself to meet her gaze. "I tried to talk him out of marrying you. I'm sorry, Shelly. I thought he was crazy to rush into things. I all but told him he had no clue what he was doing. But I was wrong. I never should have tried to talk him out of marrying you. But I did, and we argued, and then ten minutes later, he was dead."

"Oh, no," she whispered, covering her mouth with her hand. "I had no idea."

"Yeah, well, it's the truth. Finding you and Ty felt like the least I could do to make up for Mark's death. I don't expect you to forgive me for my actions that night. I can't find a way to forgive myself. I'm not sure why I thought I could replace Mark in Ty's life."

Shelly shook her head. "It's not your fault."

He wasn't listening. "I suck at relationships. I always have. I'll never be able to replace Ty's father. Only the man you fall in love with, the man you eventually marry has that right." The truth spoken so boldly tore at his heart. He'd fallen in love with Shelly. Yet, he also knew he was the last man on the planet she'd ever love in return. "If I hadn't interfered, you and Mark would be happily married by now."

Shelly didn't say anything to that, and he didn't blame her. After a moment, she turned and left the office, closing the door behind her.

Confessing his role in Mark's death should have made him feel better.

But it didn't.

SHELLY WALKED BRISKLY through Lifeline's hangar, practically running by the time she was outside. Her breath heaved from her lungs as she searched for her car.

A cramp in her side had her doubling over, gasping with pain. Why was she running? You couldn't run from your memories. Hadn't she learned that the hard way?

You and Mark would be happily married by now.

Jared's words echoed in her mind. They weren't true, but she hadn't been able to find the words or the courage to tell him.

When she could breathe, she drew in a deep lungful of air and tried to clear the haunting memories away. She didn't have time for this. To stand here thinking about Mark. About Jared. About the real reason Jared had tracked her down. She didn't want to empathize with him or understand him.

And most of all, she didn't want to hear about how badly Jared longed to play the role of father figure in Ty's life.

She turned in a complete circle, unable to remember where she'd parked. There. She saw her car and ran toward it. After sliding behind the wheel, she drove back to Children's Memorial, doing her best to calm her nerves before making her way back to Ty's room.

Her hands were shaking when she opened the door. She pasted a bright smile on her face. "I'm back."

"Did you get your schedule worked out?" Ellen wanted to know.

"Yes. Wednesday and Thursday. If you're sure you're okay with watching him."

"Perfectly fine. The pin care is easy-peasy. And I'm sure Alex will appreciate having his friend back." Ellen smiled as she motioned for her son to get off Ty's bed. "Come on, Alex. We need to go."

"Aw, Mom, why?" Alex acted as if he'd been separated from Ty for months rather than a few days.

"Because I said so." Ellen rolled her eyes at Shelly. "Emma is probably ripping Daddy's hair out as we speak."

A smile tugged at the corner of Shelly's mouth as she pictured Ellen's husband Jeff playing dolls and dress-up with Emma.

She could easily imagine Jared doing the same thing.

Stop it. Jared would have his own children one day. He

didn't suck at relationships. He'd been wonderful to her until . . .

Whatever. It didn't matter.

She walked Ellen and Alex to the door, giving Ellen a quick hug of thanks as she left. As her friend walked away, Shelly noticed another familiar woman walking toward her.

Jared's mother. She quickly closed Ty's door, standing in front of it like a sentinel guarding the gate.

"Hello, Shelly." Elizabeth didn't seem the least bit daunted at Shelly's militant posture. "I'm glad to see you. I'd like to talk to you, alone."

Shelly lifted her chin. "I'm not sure we have anything to discuss."

"That's where you're wrong." Elizabeth's smile faded. "I know I did you a grave injustice six years ago, and I'd like to make amends. I think it's time I learned more about the woman my son loved enough to marry."

14

The sick feeling in Shelly's stomach quadrupled in force. Obviously, Jared's mother didn't know the truth either. No one did.

And Shelly wasn't anxious to be the one to enlighten her.

"Honestly, this isn't necessary." Shelly struggled to maintain her composure.

"I think it is." Elizabeth glanced up and down the hospital corridor. "We can talk here or go someplace more private—it's up to you."

Shelly hesitated, then reluctantly gave in. "I need a minute to let Ty know I'll be gone for a bit."

Elizabeth nodded, and Shelly was surprised the woman didn't insist on going into Ty's room with her. She ducked her head inside the door to find him engrossed in a children's movie on the television. Children's Memorial had a cable channel that catered to kids, which was perfect. "Ty, I need to take a walk for a few minutes, will you be okay while I'm gone?"

"Sure." He barely spared her a look, his gaze riveted on the television

"Great, I'll be back soon."

Elizabeth was waiting when she closed the door to Ty's room behind her. Shelly led the way to the small visitor's lounge at the end of the hallway.

"Mrs. O'Connor—" Shelly began.

"Oh please, call me Elizabeth." For the first time, Shelly noticed the older woman nervously twisting her wedding ring on her finger. "After all, you were practically my daughter-in-law."

Oh boy. Shelly rubbed her damp palms against her denim jeans. This was going to be worse than she'd thought.

"Besides, I need to apologize for my behavior that night six years ago." Elizabeth's voice wavered. "Try to understand, I was out of my mind with grief when you arrived. To lose a child . . ." She swallowed hard, then continued, "I only pray you never have to experience what I went through that night."

Shelly glanced down at her hands, knowing exactly what Elizabeth was talking about. Fear of losing your child was all-consuming and not even close to actually living through the loss. If anything happened to Ty . . . she couldn't complete the thought. As horrible as that night had been, it was easier now to understand the woman's motive.

"I hope so, too," she murmured.

"There now, stop it or we'll both be blubbering." Elizabeth took out a crumpled tissue, dabbed at her eyes, then blew her nose daintily.

Shelly couldn't help but smile as she swiped her fingers beneath her eyes. "I know what you mean. I don't think I ever cried until I had Tyler."

"Exactly. Kids have a way of doing that to you, even

when they're older." Elizabeth sighed in relief. "I'm glad you can understand and accept my apology. I want to welcome you and Ty into our family."

Shelly's smile faded. "You're being very kind, Mrs. O'Connor, I mean, Elizabeth, but I think there's something you should know." She paused, then forced herself to be honest. "Mark did propose to me the night he found out I was pregnant. But I never agreed to marry him."

Elizabeth's eyes widened. "What do you mean? What did you say to him?"

"I didn't say anything. Frankly, I was so overwhelmed over the idea of having a baby before I'd manage to graduate with my nursing degree that I couldn't even comprehend Mark's proposal." She forced herself to meet Elizabeth's gaze head-on.

"That's okay, dear." Elizabeth reached over to pat her hand in a soothing gesture. "I understand."

"No, I don't think you do." Shelly drew in a deep breath, then said in a rush, "I want you to know I cared about Mark. Very much. But we'd jumped into the physical part of our relationship too quickly, and I soon realized that we were better off as friends. That night—" It was forever engraved in her memory. "He assumed my silence was agreement, but in fact, I knew I couldn't do it. I couldn't marry him. Because you see, I didn't love him."

Elizabeth was apparently stunned speechless.

"I'm sorry," Shelly said, feeling helpless. "But now you know that I was never going to be your daughter-in-law. But I do understand your desire to see Tyler. As long as we can agree on terms, I won't stand in your way."

"I think I can work with that." Elizabeth still looked as if she was knocked off balance at what Shelly had revealed. "Thank you."

"You're welcome. Now if you don't mind, I'd like to get back to Tyler." Shelly quickly rose to her feet and headed back to her son's room.

Elizabeth didn't follow.

Shelly knew Mark had been at Stephan's that night, hadn't he always? And of course, he'd had a few drinks. She shouldn't have sprung the news of her pregnancy on him like that, but she'd needed someone to talk to. Mark had shocked her with his instant proposal, so much so that she hadn't been able to bring herself to answer him. He hadn't pushed but had quickly left, saying something about talking to his family and getting things lined up for their future.

Had Mark seen the truth about her feelings reflected in her eyes? She'd always wondered but had never known for certain. It was part of the reason she'd written to him so often in her journal.

Jared blamed himself for Mark's death, but Shelly knew with deep certainty that the fault was equally hers.

LATE ON WEDNESDAY NIGHT, Jared entered Lifeline's lounge to find Shelly seated on the sofa, her head tipped back, her eyes closed. She looked pale and drawn, obviously exhausted, but achingly lovely.

Just like the moment he'd first seen her.

He longed to gather her close, smooth away the lines of fatigue with a kiss. But she wasn't his to hold. Seeing her like this, close enough to touch, made Jared wonder if he needed to tender his resignation. Not seeing Shelly would be less torturous than working with her on a daily basis, knowing exactly what he was missing.

He shouldn't have offered to switch shifts with Evans,

but the guy had wanted to spend time with his wife and newborn daughter. Jared couldn't blame the guy, he'd do the same thing if he had a family.

But he didn't. All the more reason to help out those who did.

As if sensing his presence, Shelly's eyes opened and her gaze locked on his. Guilty of gawking again, Jared inwardly groaned.

"Jared." She sat up, blinking in confusion. "What time is it?"

"Just after midnight." He knew how disoriented she felt. Working swing shifts could really mess with your brain. "Don't worry, you didn't sleep through the shift. It's been a quiet night."

"Shh, don't say the Q word," Shelly cautioned superstitiously.

Too late. Their pages went off simultaneously. "I shouldn't have opened my big mouth," he said on a sigh.

Shelly looked at her pager. "It's a motor vehicle crash involving teenagers." She grimaced. "They're requesting adult and pediatric response, which doesn't sound good."

"Let's go."

Reese had the chopper revved up and ready to fly in less than two minutes, and they were airborne in less than five. A hard knot formed in Jared's belly as the chopper banked and headed for the scene. Motor vehicle crashes, especially at night, always reminded him of Mark.

The scene was bad, though no worse than he'd expected. They were immediately flagged toward one car, or what appeared to be half a car. The other half was crumpled beyond recognition.

"We managed to get two teens out after a lengthy extraction. To be honest, we thought they were dead, but they weren't. The sixteen-year-old boy was driving, but the girl is younger. Has a high school ID in her purse but no driver's license or temporary permit."

He and Shelly split up, Jared instinctively taking the driver. The paramedic had just started CPR. Jared felt for a pulse and nodded at the paramedic. "Good pulse with CPR."

"Do you want me to hold off for a moment?" the paramedic asked.

Jared nodded. The boy's pulse immediately vanished. Not good. "No pulse, we need to continue resuscitation."

"I will but check his pupils. They were dilated when I pulled him out of the vehicle."

Jared examined the boy's pupils and immediately noticed they blown, a sure sign of severe head trauma. No way was this kid going to make it. Still, they had to keep going. "We need to hyperventilate him, maybe that will give him a chance."

But it was no use. Even after a solid thirty minutes of resuscitation, the kid never responded. For a long moment, he and the paramedics stared down at the dead boy.

Sixteen was far too young to die. But all the emergency medicine in the world couldn't save everyone. It hadn't saved Mark either.

Jared shook off the desolation before crossing over to where Shelly knelt beside her patient.

"Come on, stay with me," Shelly said, delivering shocks at what appeared to be ventricular fibrillation on the portable monitor.

He dropped to his knees on the other side of her. "I'll get an intracardiac needle. I think she has cardiac tamponade."

"I tried to tap her once but wasn't successful." Shelly

gave yet another shock, then began doing CPR while he grabbed the six-inch needle.

"Hold CPR."

Shelly stopped and pulled the girl's blouse out of the way so he could insert the cardiac needle. At first he didn't get anything, so he changed the angle and tried again. This time, the syringe filled with blood.

"Yes!" Shelly cried. "You did it."

The girl's cardiac rhythm returned, and with one meaningful glance, they understood they needed to get her into the helicopter for an immediate transfer to the hospital.

"Children's Memorial?" Shelly asked.

He estimated the girl was roughly fifteen and based on her heart issues would need a cardiac surgeon. Based on her adult size, he shook his head. "No, let's go to Trinity Medical Center. The adult cardiac surgeons need to take her to the OR as soon as possible."

Reese had the chopper ready to go. He and Shelly quickly loaded the young teen inside. Twice Jared pulled more blood from the pericardial sac around her heart, and he knew she must have an arterial laceration. He called to make sure there would be a cardiac surgeon waiting for them when they landed.

"What's the problem?" The surgeon glanced at him expectantly.

"Repeated cardiac tamponade, I think she has a lacerated artery."

"I'll take her to the OR," the surgeon agreed. "Where are her parents?"

"Not sure. The cops at the scene of the accident were tracking them down."

The surgeon nodded and whisked the girl to the OR with a bevy of ER personnel. The ones remaining behind asked about the second victim. Jared informed them the driver of the vehicle didn't make it.

"Brittany! Where's my daughter!"

Jared turned to see a hysterical woman flying through the doorway. Two nurses approached on either side, but for some reason, the woman's wild eyes locked on his.

"Where's my daughter?"

"Easy now, she's alive and in surgery." Shelly's calm voice seemed to penetrate the woman's hysteria.

"Surgery? What kind of surgery?"

"There was a problem with her heart, but we have the best surgeon taking care of her." Shelly put her arm around the woman's shoulders. "Now listen, you need to calm down so that we can get your daughter's information from you, understand?"

"Yes. Brittany, my baby." The woman's face crumpled. "We had a fight, and I thought she was in bed, but then I discovered she sneaked out of her room to meet with that boyfriend of hers. The last words to her were said in anger. What if I never get the chance to tell her I love her? What if she dies thinking I hated her?" The woman broke down sobbing, leaning heavily on Shelly for support.

He braced her on the other side so they could get the crying woman into a nearby chair. Then he stepped back, watching as Shelly comforted Brittany's mother, reassuring her that she'd have a second chance with her daughter.

Jared wasn't so sure that was entirely true. He knew better than anyone that there wasn't always a second chance to right a wrong.

He hadn't been given one with Mark.

～

WHILE SHELLY FINISHED CONSOLING Brittany's mother, Jared called the paramedic base to let them know their transport was finished. It was close to three in the morning—only four more hours to go until the end of the shift. The base radioed Reese who decided to take the opportunity to refuel. Jared agreed to meet up with the pilot on the helipad in thirty minutes.

He mentally thanked the ED nurses who had freshly brewed coffee in the employee lounge. Shelly joined him there a few minutes later.

"Smells great," she said, heading straight for the pot.

"Tastes just as good as it smells." He eyed her over the rim of his mug. "Is Brittany's mom going to be all right?"

Shelly's smile slid sideways. "If her daughter survives surgery. Otherwise, I'm not so sure."

Jared nodded. "It's not smart to offer false hope."

She scowled and carefully set her mug down. "What do you mean?"

"There aren't always second chances. I argued with Mark, and then he died. There isn't anything I can do to change that."

She stared at him intently. "What if I told you it was my fault? Would you forgive me?"

"Yes, of course, but that's not the point. Mark's death was my fault, not yours. I'm the one who argued with him, told him he was crazy to quit school and marry you."

"I didn't love him," she blurted. "Mark asked me to marry him, but I didn't answer. Because I knew I couldn't. I didn't love him, Jared. And I think he saw the truth in my eyes, and that's why he rushed out to see you."

Jared frowned, thinking back to that fateful night. "Mark was certain the two of you were getting married. In fact, I specifically asked him if he loved you and he said yes."

She winced and glanced away. "He thought he loved me, but he was just being nice. In my opinion, he was using the baby as an excuse to quit law school. To write full time. Trust me, we would not have gotten married. So you see, his death was as much my fault as anyone else's. If you can forgive me, you'll have to forgive yourself."

"I'm not sure . . ." His voice petered out as she stepped closer.

Shelly took the half-empty coffee cup from his hands and set it aside so she could hold both of his hands in hers. He marveled at her small hands, firm as if infused with the strength of Wonder Woman.

"I think after tonight I believe in second chances, Jared." Shelly's voice was soft. "Think about what Brittany's mother said, about parting in anger. Life is too short to hold a grudge. Isn't that what carrying guilt amounts to? If the situation was reversed, you'd forgive me. So what is it that you're really blaming Mark for?"

For dying? The realization hit hard, stunning him as if he'd been hit square in the gut. He blamed Mark for drinking and driving. For putting their family through so much grief.

For leaving Shelly to raise their son, Tyler, alone.

"I—don't blame Mark." The words sounded uncertain to his own ears. "I blame myself for not supporting him."

"And he should have been responsible not to drink and drive." Shelly voiced the concern he struggled with the most. "I cared about Mark, as you did. But that doesn't mean he was perfect. None of us are. So if it's okay for Mark to do some things wrong, then it's okay for us, too."

How was it that she made sense out of chaos? Suddenly everything was crystal clear. He couldn't blame his dead brother for making a bad choice, so he'd focused on his role in the events of that night.

"You're right, Shelly." Jared had played a role, as had Shelly. But Mark's behavior had been the ultimate cause of the crash. Jared felt as if a heavy weight was lifted off his shoulders. He tugged on Shelly's hands, pulling her close. She wrapped her arms around his waist, and he inhaled deeply, filling his head with her fresh lilac scent. "Life is too short to hold a grudge. I've seen enough death to know that. Guilt blinded me from seeing the truth."

"For me, too," Shelly acknowledged. She drew back enough to meet his gaze. "I was wrong to get angry with you, Jared. I treated you badly for bringing your parents here. And I never told you how thankful I am for your kindness in donating your blood for Ty's surgery."

"I'm the one who needs to apologize." Jared lifted a hand to smooth a strand of hair from her cheek. "Donating blood was nothing, I'd do anything for you and Ty. I'm sorry that my parents showed up without an invitation, but please know I didn't encourage that. I told them to wait. But the end result was the same anyway."

"Your mother isn't too bad," Shelly admitted.

"She means well. And I let her and my dad have it when I heard what they did to you." He stared deeply into her eyes. *Tell her*, the tiny voice in the back of his head shouted. *Tell her how much you love her, you idiot! Don't chicken out now!*

"Oh, Jared." Her eyes misted, and his heart sank. Was this the same expression she'd given Mark? Was she telling him right now that she could never love him?

Before he could risk everything by telling her how he felt, their pagers went off. As much as he was tempted to throw the blasted thing against the room, Shelly pulled away from him to reach for hers.

"Reese has finished refueling." Shelly frowned. "Huh. I didn't even realize he'd gone. He's ready to head back to the hangar."

"Yeah, I told him we'd meet him on the helipad." He didn't want to go, he wanted to stay and continue talking to Shelly.

They still had unfinished business between them. At least on his part.

"Oh, sure." She blinked and gestured toward the door leading out of the lounge. "We'd better go up to meet him. What time is it anyway?"

"Time I told you the truth." Jared caught her hand in his before she could completely slip away. The staff lounge wasn't the most romantic place on earth, but he couldn't let it go. The next page could be a call out. "I love you, Shelly. I fell in love with you the moment I saw you dancing around your house, blowing that silly horn, and wearing the goofy hat while celebrating Ty's health. I know you're strong and independent. I know you don't need anyone's help, but I need you. Will you please marry me?"

She gaped at him for a long moment. The hope that had filled his heart melted away as he realized she was trying to find a way to let him down slowly.

But then she tightened her grip on his hands. "Jared, you're wrong. I do need you. You have no idea how much. These past few days have been horrible without you. You think I'm strong? What a joke. I'm so not."

"You worked part-time to get yourself through school, had a child without any help financial or otherwise, moved back to your hometown, even though you didn't have any family left to help support you, yet still managed to become a flight nurse." Jared lifted a brow. "Being raised by well-off parents and attending medical school seems insignificant compared to all of that."

She rolled her eyes and laughed. "Hardly, but you didn't let me finish. I love you, too. I realized how much when you put on the same goofy hat and joined our dance party. Yes. I'd be honored to be your wife."

"Thank goodness, Shelly." He buried his face in her hair, clutching her close. "You had me worried for a moment that you were going to turn me down."

Their pagers went off again. Shelly pulled away with a loud sigh. "Reese is getting impatient. We'd better go."

"Yes, but in less than four hours, our shift will be over. I know we both need to get some rest, but I'd like to come over later to have dinner with you and Ty."

"I'd like that, too." Her response made him grin.

He kept his arm around her waist as they left the nurses lounge. On the elevator ride up to the helipad that was shared between Trinity Medical Center and Children's Memorial, he glanced down at her.

"Do you think Ty will mind when we tell him the news?"

"He'll be thrilled," Shelly confided. "He's always wanted a father, and you've been included in his nightly prayers since the day you two met."

"Really?" He was touched to hear that Ty had included him in his prayers from the very beginning.

Before the elevator doors opened, he pulled her close and kissed her. An embrace full of pent-up desire and long-ing, one that held a silent promise for their future. When the elevator doors opened, he broke off their kiss to whisper, "Without you, I'd never have believed in second chances."

Reese stood outside on the helipad beside his chopper, standing close to the building to shelter from the wind. His gaze narrowed on them with annoyance. "What in the world took you so long? I'm freezing my butt off up here."

Shelly walked over and leaned up to press a kiss to Reese's cheek. "Don't be angry, Reese. Congratulate us. Jared and I are getting married."

"Well, well." Reese's anger faded, and he clapped a hand on Jared's shoulder, shaking his head in bemusement at the radiant expression on Shelly's face. "That's great news. Especially since I'm pretty sure I just won twenty-five bucks in the dating pool."

Dear Reader,

Many of you know I'm a nurse by day and an author by night. I was fortunate enough to do a ride along on our hospital's Flight For Life helicopter, a truly amazing experience. From that one flight, this entire series was born. *A Doctor's Promise* is the first book in the Lifeline Air Rescue series.

I hope you enjoyed Jared and Shelly's story. If you're interested in more Lifeline stories, I have the first chapter of *A Doctor's Secret* included here for your reading pleasure.

Reviews are very important to authors, so if you liked this story, I would very much appreciate if you took the time to leave a review on the platform where you purchased it.

I always enjoy hearing from my readers. I can be found through my website at https://www.laurascottbooks.com, on Facebook at Laura Scott Author, or on Twitter @laurascottbooks. If you're interested in hearing about my new releases, sign up for my newsletter. I offer a free novella for all newsletter subscribers.

Until next time,

Laura Scott

A DOCTOR'S SECRET

Chapter One

"Two minutes till landing."

Dr. Samantha Kearn took a deep breath as Reese Jarvis's calm, steady voice flowed through her headset. The Lifeline helicopter pilot could have made a living as a radio announcer playing late-night love songs. His voice reminded her of hot sultry nights, in contrast to the harsh, cold winter day she was stuck flying in.

At least she was flying.

This was it. Her first solo flight as the physician in charge. Only five more months of her residency to go and she'd graduate to a full-time attending physician. Reese landed the helicopter gently, without so much as a thud. For a moment she hesitated, her hand on the door. What if she messed up?

With a sudden burst of determination, Samantha pushed the door open and jumped to the ground. She wouldn't screw up. She was confident in her training. And maybe she was finally putting her past behind her, too.

With renewed vigor, she followed Andrew, the flight paramedic on board, and helped him slide the gurney from the hatch in the back of the chopper.

Samantha's sweeping gaze gauged the distance from the helicopter to the building. The small community hospital didn't have a rooftop helipad; they would be forced to cross the expansive and mostly empty surface parking lot to find the hospital entrance and then finally the intensive care unit.

She'd already gotten a brief report from the ICU attending physician. Her patient was Jamie Armon, a thirty-eight-year-old woman who had originally come in with flu-like symptoms which had grown increasingly worse over the next several days. Fearing there was something more complex wrong with her, they'd requested a transfer to a larger, tertiary care hospital.

Samantha impatiently tapped her foot as the elevator rambled to the third floor. Andrew noticed and offered a wan smile.

"Almost there."

She nodded. "I know." What she didn't know was how their patient was doing.

Inside the hospital's small ICU, her first glance at the monitor over the patient's bedside made her heart sink. As a rule, patients needed to be stable prior to transport, but right now, Jamie's heart rate and blood pressure teetered on the edge of a very steep canyon.

Samantha steeled her resolve. No way was she going to lose her first patient on her first solo flight.

"How much dopamine to you have her on?" She looked at the nurse as Andrew began switching all the IV connections to their smaller, compact transport models.

"Not sure, maybe around seven micrograms per kilo per

minute, maybe a little more." The Cedar Ridge Hospital nurse appeared flustered as she thrust a stack of printed paperwork at Andrew.

Samantha felt a flash of pity. Smaller hospitals didn't get a lot of experience with very sick and complicated patients. From what she could tell, the nurse wasn't getting much support from the physician either. No wonder she was frazzled.

"Let me see." Samantha looked at the bag, then at the pump for the rate. She quickly did the math, verifying the patient was getting twice as much as the nurse had told her. "She's over the maximum limit, has her blood pressure always been that low?"

"Yes. No matter how high I titrate the medication, her blood pressure won't budge. The doctors here aren't even sure what's wrong with her." The nurse's bloodshot eyes were wide with anxiety.

"What are her labs?" Samantha took the paperwork from Andrew and paged through it. "She needs more volume. Double the rate of her maintenance fluids. She's low on potassium, too. Do you have a supplement we can hang before we go?"

The nurse nodded. "I'll get it."

Samantha wanted to see the radiology results, but they didn't actually print them on film anymore. When the nurse returned, Andrew took the supplement and hung it on the IV pole he'd already set up on their equipment.

"Pull up her most recent X-ray," Samantha ordered.

"I'm not sure it's been read yet." The nurse fiddled with the controls on the bedside computer until the image bloomed on the screen. "We took it ten minutes ago after placing a new central line."

The picture was grainy and not as clear as Samantha

would have liked. She filed the information on the new line away and glanced at Andrew. There wasn't anything more they could do other than to get this patient to Trinity Medical Center as soon as possible. "Okay, let's go."

She and Andrew packed Jamie up and quickly wheeled her out to the waiting helicopter. The wind was bitterly cold, and Samantha tugged the blanket more securely around their patient.

With Andrew's help, they loaded the patient into the chopper, then climbed in after her. As soon as they were settled with their helmets on, Reese asked, "Are you ready back there?"

"Good to go," Samantha confirmed, before placing the extra pair of headphones on Jamie's head. They were necessary in order to communicate with her, although Jamie appeared to be pretty much out of it. Even as she watched, Jamie's blood pressure dipped lower.

Reese was conversing with local air traffic control, giving coordinates for their flight plan, so she waited until he was finished.

"Reese, what's the fastest you can get us to Trinity?" As she spoke, she increased the dopamine medication, knowing it wasn't going to help much since it was maxed out. The knot in her belly tightened. If the blood pressure didn't respond, she'd have to add another vasopressor.

"We have the north wind behind us now, so we should be able to make it back to Milwaukee in forty minutes. A light snow is beginning to fall, though, so I may have to fly at a lower altitude to avoid the freezing rain. It will add time to the trip."

Normally the idea of flying in freezing rain bothered her. She'd learned in her training how ice coating the blades could down a chopper faster than a clay pigeon. But Reese's voice was so unflappably steady, she didn't argue. "Do what you can to get us safely to Trinity as soon as possible."

"Roger that." Reese lifted the chopper off the ground and gently banked to the left.

"Hey, Dr. Kearn, I'm not feeling a pulse." Andrew was holding his fingers on Jamie's carotid artery.

Samantha wanted to tell Reese to go back, but that wasn't an option. She pulled the blankets aside and noticed the skin along the entire left side of the patient's chest, the same side with the new central line, was puffy, the tissue clearly filling with air. Just then, the chopper took a hard bump. As she was unbelted and perched on the edge of the bench seat, Samantha almost fell face-first onto the patient.

"Sorry, are you all right back there?" Reese's even tone eased her alarm, calming her shaky nerves.

"Yes, but we have a problem. She's crashing. Can you hold this thing steady?"

"If I need to slow down and lower my altitude, I will," was his immediate response.

"I need to insert a chest tube; she has a tension pneumothorax." Samantha quickly dug in the flight bag for the necessary equipment. Maybe she should have waited back at the hospital, requesting a better chest X-ray before leaving the ICU with their patient.

She hoped and prayed her error didn't cost this patient her life.

"Now?" Andrew's voice rose an octave. "I've never done an in-flight chest tube."

"Watch closely, because we're doing one now." Samantha didn't let on how she'd never performed the procedure at thousands of feet in the air either.

"Okay, I'm reducing altitude," Reese informed them.

The helicopter's flight smoothed out. Samantha took a

large bore needle and catheter and quickly inserted it between the patient's fourth and fifth ribs. Jamie moaned and flinched beneath her hands. Andrew managed to connect the small portable suction machine to the end of the catheter.

"I have a pulse." Samantha couldn't prevent the wave of relief. Thank goodness the chest tube worked.

"Blood pressure is up, too." Andrew sounded content as he sat back in his seat. "You did it."

"Yes, we did." They were a team, and Samantha was grateful for it.

"Do you need me to divert to a closer facility?" Reese asked a few minutes later.

To veer off course to request an emergency standby landing was rare. Most pilots would rather push on to their scheduled destination. She wasn't surprised to discover Reese was the type of pilot who would do whatever was necessary for their patient.

"No, thanks. We can make it to Trinity." Samantha busied her hands with double-checking every connection, readjusting the medication rates, all in an effort to hide the fact that her hands were shaking. She wondered if Andrew had any idea how close their patient had come to dying.

"ETA twenty-five minutes." Reese's steady voice filled her helmet. "Just let me know if you need anything. I'm climbing back up another five hundred feet."

"Her pressure is dropping again," Andrew said, concern lacing his tone.

"I'm going to place a new line. I'm not convinced the one they put in is any good."

"What can I do?" This time, Andrew seemed determined to help rather than freak out.

"Prep the right side of her chest." She pulled out a new central line kit and sterile gloves.

"Dr. Kearn, do you need me to reduce altitude again?"

She was surprised to hear Reese address her so formally but was thankful he was paying attention to what was going on with their patient. The situation was still tenuous, but his reassuring voice remained her anchor.

"If you could." Somewhere along the way her fingers had stopped shaking and she was able to insert the needle and find the subclavian vein without difficulty. *That's it*, she told herself. *Just pretend you're in the ED where you completed months of training. See? No problem.*

Within minutes, she had the new line placed.

"Move the drips to the new line," she told Andrew. "I have good blood return. The chest X-ray will have to wait until we land."

Moments later, Jamie's blood pressure returned to normal. Satisfied, Samantha quickly cleaned and dressed the site.

"Sounds like things are better back there," Reese said.

She found herself smiling. "They are."

"ETA fifteen minutes. Less if I put more air under our belly. There's a nice tailwind up there."

The image of Reese body surfing, flying like Superman on a wave of wind, made her smile widen. Now that the worst was over, she could afford to relax.

"Sure, why not? I like a little air under my belly. And things are good back here."

Andrew made several notations in the medical record, then reduced the rate of the dopamine drip. With the line working properly, Jamie didn't need those massive doses she'd been on when they'd picked her up.

Something the ICU attending at the hospital should have figured out for himself.

She decided against pulling out the line that wasn't working, fearing that it would only cause uncontrolled bleeding. They were so focused on their patient that she didn't realize how much time had passed until she heard Reese's voice in her ear.

"Five minutes until landing."

"Thanks." Samantha helped Andrew prepare their patient for transport. She hit the button on her mike, signaling a call to the paramedic base. "Lifeline to paramedic base, please let Trinity's ICU staff know that we need a chest X-ray completed upon arrival. A new central line was placed in the right subclavian vein."

"Roger Lifeline."

Reese landed the helicopter with finesse on the rooftop helipad at Trinity Medical Center. Samantha waited until Reese gave them the all clear before jumping out to unload their patient.

As promised, the portable chest X-ray machine was waiting for them in the ICU. The digital reading proved the line she'd placed was in the correct place and verified the original line had gone through the vein. Even better, the air pocket in Jamie's lungs was already resolving.

Relieved, Samantha watched the ICU team work on Jamie, a woman only eight years her senior. Now that she'd handed over Jamie's care, the seriousness of the situation hit hard. This poor young woman had almost died up there. Thank heavens, she'd recognized the problem early enough to fix it.

"Nice job, Dr. Kearn." Andrew pulled the gurney out into the hall. "Ready to go?"

"Yeah." She wasn't really, but of course, her work here

was finished. She'd survived her first solo flight. Surely, they'd get easier from here on out. Now, if only she could find a way to get the rest of her personal life on track.

One step at a time. You have a new apartment, and you've just about finished your training, only five more months to go. You finally have your independence. Be thankful for what you have.

Once they were back on the rooftop landing pad, she and Andrew headed over to where Reese waited with the chopper.

She frowned when she noticed that Reese had shut the machine down. He stood outside the helicopter, his expression grim as he stared at the aircraft.

"What's wrong?" Samantha asked.

"Ice on the blades. It's amazing we made it here in one piece. We'll have to de-ice before we can return to the Lifeline Air Rescue hangar."

Reese's thigh muscles quivered with the effort of keeping himself upright as the bones in his legs seemingly disintegrated into dust. His face felt frozen, but he couldn't relax. He refused to let the rest of the crew know how badly this had shaken him.

They'd almost crashed.

In fact, he had no idea why they hadn't.

Red dots swam before his eyes until he feared he would end up much like the unconscious patient they'd just unloaded minutes earlier. He didn't want to believe what he'd seen, but the vision of the ice-covered blades was indelibly etched in his brain.

He'd noticed the slightest change in the stick as they'd

landed. He wanted to claim instinct had forced him to double-check the chopper blades, but in truth, he'd been following routine training that was drilled into every pilot.

Five minutes longer and they certainly would have crashed. Or at the very least been forced into a hard landing.

Was this how Valerie had felt in those moments before the crash? And Greg? Had his best friend noticed the slight hesitation of the stick mid-flight or had the blades just stopped spinning?

Did he really want to know what had gone through his fiancée's and best friend's minds before they'd died?

The frankly curious gazes of Samantha and Andrew, watching as he de-iced the chopper, was all that kept him from sinking to his knees.

"Reese, do you need help?"

Samantha's lyrical sweet voice helped strengthen his resolve not to show his weakness. *Dr. Kearn to you, dummy,* he chided himself. The lady was smart, cool under pressure, and she deserved his respect, not his overly familiar thoughts. He didn't turn around but sensed rather than heard her come up behind him. A light evergreen scent teased his nostrils, kicking his pulse into high gear. The metallic taste of fear faded, quickly replaced by the slightest stirring of desire.

"No, thanks. I'll be finished in a few minutes." His voice sounded wooden to his ears, but hopefully Samantha wouldn't notice.

Dr. Kearn. Get it through your concrete-lined skull, she's Dr. Kearn!

"This is a first for me, being grounded to de-ice," she admitted softly, stepping into the line of his peripheral vision. "I guess it's better to be safe than sorry."

No, it was better to be safe than *dead*. The living were the only ones who were sorry. Reese mentally drew himself back on track. No sense in scaring the daylights out of the rest of the crew. Better that he kept his dark thoughts to himself.

"There, I'm finished." He verified the chemicals had performed their magic and pronounced the helicopter back in flying form. "I'll put this stuff away, then we can board."

"Reese?"

Bracing himself, he slowly turned to face her. For a moment he couldn't speak. She was so beautiful, no matter how hard she tried not to be. She'd caught his eye that very first day, her glorious red hair pulled into a no-nonsense braid and her creamy complexion free of makeup. She appeared oblivious to the male attention she drew from the other paramedics and physician crew members. Several pilots had commented about her, wondering about her availability, but Reese noticed she never made a flirtatious gesture or remark. Almost as if she made it a point to never cross the line of polite friendliness. The "off-limits" signs couldn't have been any clearer.

Which was fine with him. He was happy enough to admire her from afar. She'd only be part of the Lifeline crew for another five months before she'd graduate to a full-fledged physician.

"Yes? What is it?" He pulled himself together with an effort.

"With the ice on the blades, how close were we to crashing?"

He hesitated, tempted to gloss over the risk, but decided he couldn't lie to her. It wasn't fair, not when her life had been on the line as much as his. "Too close."

"I see." Her eyebrows drew together to form a solemn line. "Thanks for telling me."

He nearly groaned. Why couldn't she just yell at him or something? He deserved that much. He was the captain of the ship. And he'd almost gotten her killed.

"Get your gear, we're ready to roll." His brusque response dimmed the sparkle in her eyes, but he told himself it was for the best. Theirs was a professional relationship, nothing more. He quickly stashed the supplies back in the hangar, then pulled the bird out of the shelter. Within moments, they were airborne once again.

The return ride was less than ten minutes, but there was an obvious lack of chatter amongst the crew as he set the helicopter on the ground. He gave Samantha and Andrew the signal to disembark, then shut down the engine.

Reese took a few extra moments to go through the basic post-flight checklist, then headed into the Lifeline lounge. Andrew and Samantha were standing there, along with some sort of delivery man holding an flower arrangement.

"Dr. Samantha Kearn?" The guy was asking as he stared down at his clipboard.

She didn't answer right away, forcing him to look up at her. "You're Dr. Samantha Kearn?" he repeated.

She nodded.

"Flower delivery for you, ma'am. Please sign here."

He thrust the clipboard at her, and she signed the form, a careful blankness in her normally expressive gray eyes. Reese frowned. What was this about? Most women were thrilled with surprise gifts, but Samantha looked green, as if she might throw up.

"Wow, Dr. Kearn, someone loves you," Andrew teased. "Who is it from? Hey, there isn't a card."

The tiny hairs on the back of Reese's neck lifted in alarm. The delivery man thrust the cellophane-wrapped flower at her, but Samantha quickly pulled her hands away, stumbling backward out of reach. When she regained her footing, she gestured to the table. "No, ah, set it there, please."

There was something wrong with this picture. Reese recognized pure fright when he saw it. In fact, Samantha looked as awful as he'd felt when he'd seen the ice coating the chopper blades.

"Andrew, did you file the flight paperwork yet?" He pinned the paramedic with a pointed look.

Andrew shook his head. "No, but I will."

"Good. I have my report here, too. Let's get these finished."

Andrew took the not too subtle hint and obediently left the lounge. Reese followed more slowly. At the doorway, he hesitated, then turned to walk back inside, just in time to see Samantha gingerly pick up the flower, still encased in plastic wrap and hurtle it into the metal trash can in the corner. A loud crash reverberated through the room.

Definitely, something wrong.

"Who sent it?" Reese asked softly. He wasn't just being nosy, he could feel Samantha's tension all the way across the room. He suddenly wanted to protect her from whoever was bothering her.

She spun around to face him, swallowed hard, then squared her shoulders, bravely meeting his gaze. "There wasn't a card."

"Still, you know who sent it, don't you?"

She remained stubbornly silent, but the guilty flash and abrupt lowering of her eyes was answer enough.

ALSO BY LAURA SCOTT

A Doctor's Secret

A Doctor's Dilemma

A Doctor's Trust

35726371R00103

Made in the USA
Lexington, KY
06 April 2019